Waterbound

Waterbound

JANE STEMP

Dial Books / *New York*

First published in the United States 1996
by Dial Books
A Division of Penguin Books USA Inc.
375 Hudson Street
New York, New York 10014

Published in Great Britain in 1995
by Hodder Children's Books
Copyright © 1995 by Jane Stemp
All rights reserved
Designed by Pamela Darcy
Printed in the U.S.A./First Edition
10 9 8 7 6 5 4 3 2 1

Library of Congress Cataloging in Publication Data
Stemp, Jane.
Waterbound/by Jane Stemp.—1st ed.   p.   cm.
Summary: In a futuristic society sixteen-year-old
Gem discovers that a group of people who call themselves
the Waterbound live hidden beneath the City.
ISBN 0–8037–1994–9 (trade)   [1. Science fiction.
2. Handicapped—Fiction. 3. Values—Fiction.] I. Title.
PZ7.S8284Wat 1996 [Fic]—dc20 95-50534 CIP AC

To my parents and my brothers.
Also in memory of Georgina.
And thanks to Nabil Shaban for
letting me preach the Fifth Gospel.

Waterbound

1

The Flower

The stream ran in under Gem's feet as she stood at City Edge; she hung herself half upside down over the wall to see where it went. Nothing but a curve like braided light as it disappeared into the dark: a very small stream for the great arch of City Bridge.

Gem righted herself and fished in her pockets. "Oh, *no!*" Today of all days. She had forgotten her card—and the key for Outside that Pa had given her the credit to buy. Gem screwed up her eyes trying to remember: a vivid mental picture of the small zinc-and-copper disc lying in the exact middle of her bed. A long walk back home, so Gem looked along City Edge to the gate. No one in sight. She walked back a little way, ran forward, and leaped for the top of the fence. Grab, scramble, kick, thud. Illicitly Outside, on her first day as a Responsible

Adult. Sixteen years and one day old, laying herself open to a two-hundred fine for walking on the environment without paying.

So this was Outside. Outside, where Admin wouldn't let you go until you were old enough and responsible enough not to damage it; Outside, where the grass was real, and not a waste of valuable food space. Gem felt as if a thin, transparent skin dropped off her. She could breathe, run, do what she liked; she ran away from the City, upstream.

The sun was beginning to go down when she strolled back toward City Bridge. It was time to wonder how she was going to get Inside again. Gem sat down by the stream.

And there was the flower. Bright red, lying on its side in the water, spinning. Beautiful. Moving fast. She flung herself forward—"Ow!"—and reached for it. Missed completely.

Gem lay on her front in the grass and watched the flower follow the curve of the stream over into the darkness. This was the only wild water near the City. Even the rain was tamed the minute it hit the ground. Piped, bottled, gathered into cisterns; recycled from the sewerage. Anything but free. Gem got up on her knees and dabbled her fingers in the water. It even seemed fresher to touch than what came out of the taps. Her long, fair hair swung forward across her face.

"Go on, you can walk right into it if you like."

"Jay! You made me jump."

He stood beside her, a long way up to look: Jay Delaiah, who was at least a year older than her and had been Outside before. "Not educating yourself?" he asked sardonically.

"I've been studying over quota for a month—"

"The girl's mad."

"—to earn myself a vacation. You may not have noticed, but yesterday was my sixteenth birthday."

"I notice everything to do with you," Jay said. There seemed to be no answer to that, and Gem lay down again. She never did know how to take Jay—acid one minute, honey the next. It made for a nerve-wracking friendship, and sometimes Gem wondered why she bothered.

"Did you see it?" she asked presently.

"Did I see what?"

"The red flower."

"Oh. Yes, I saw that." Jay sat down on the grass where the arch of City Bridge sprang and folded his legs carefully, one hand on each ankle. The reflected sunlight dappled his dark-brown face and vanished in the shine of his black hair.

"I wanted it," Gem said.

"Wouldn't have lasted," said Jay; and after a moment added, "I'll get you another one."

Gem looked up at him. "You mean you put it there?"

Jay shrugged and stared blandly back at her: brown eyes into blue. "Out of Ma's garden," he said.

"Why?" Gem asked.

"Why not . . . ?"

Gem rolled onto her back and looked at the sky. Clouds were drifting across it in puffs of white. For a moment she felt as if she might fall off the world. Then the clouds weren't moving but she was, drifting on the sky in her scarlet sweater. "Where does it go?" she asked.

"Where does what go?" Jay liked people to be precise. Sometimes Gem wasn't sure whether he just enjoyed the rise he got out of people by making them rephrase their questions to perfect accuracy.

"Where does the stream go?" she asked again. "After the City?"

There was so much silence that Gem sat up and stared at Jay. Had he not heard, or was he just ignoring her?

"Jay?" she said inquiringly.

"Nobody knows," he answered, his voice flat and final.

"Somebody must."

"Nobody." He stood up. "I have to go home. We must be the only ones Outside today."

Gem pulled bits of grass from her sweater. "I'll have to climb."

Jay stopped short with something between a whistle and a laugh. "Well, aren't you the one! Shall I give you a leg up?"

Gem looked at him. "I came out on my own, I can get back in, thanks." Except that there were people strolling along City Edge now. "I may have to wait."

"I have a better idea," Jay said. "Put your thumbprint on this." He flipped her an Outside key, and Gem was so astonished, she made no move to catch it.

"You have them to spare?"

"They litter the floors of Upper Admin. Pa gives me them instead of credit sometimes." Jay took another key out of his pocket. "Come on!"

Gem sniffed. "What it is to be stinking rich." But she picked up the key and pushed her thumb into it; then Jay let himself into the City with his own key, fed the spare into the entrance slot, caught it when it dropped out, and tossed it over the fence. "There," he said. "So long as nobody was watching, and they don't check the gate line and find that you went Outside only to come in again half a minute later, we're clear."

"Technology has no initiative," Gem said as she let herself in the correct way.

"No—imagination runs rings around it. Hey—don't

throw that away!" Jay caught Gem's hand. "I want it."

"But it's been used." Gem opened her hand and let the key slip into Jay's palm; but he didn't loosen his grip right away.

"I keep them." Jay slid the metal discs into his pocket and grinned. "They rattle so nicely when I play at coin economy."

"I never knew you were an antiquarian. . . ."

"You should see my collection of bookmarks."

They had sauntered up along City Edge and were leaning on the parapet over the stream.

"I wonder what it's like in the dark," Gem said.

"If you're far enough from the City, you can see the stars," Jay said. "It's very quiet. The wind in the grass, and sometimes the insects chirping. When I was Outside for the night, I woke up before dawn and heard the birds singing."

"You are so lucky," Gem said. "Anyone else would hate you."

"I can't help having my parents," Jay said. He stuck his hands into his pockets and looked down at her, his smile less sarcastic than usual. "You mind a lot, don't you?" he said. "That is, not about my parents. Just this."

"Of course I mind," Gem said, turning away from the Edge and beginning to walk toward the center of the City. Leaves, not many, blew along the water channels in the middle of the street with a dry rustling whisper. "Of course I mind," she said again. "Living between fences, always having to be careful about, quote, resources natural and human made, because people I never knew or heard of weren't—careful, I mean—and came to their senses too late."

"Better late than never," Jay said.

"What an ancient cliché."

"So why not recycle words, like everything else?"

Gem jumped down into the water channel; at the same moment, somewhere in the distance, a siren sounded.

"Now look what you've done," Jay said. "Cracked a water line."

"Never," she retorted. "That's South Four's siren. Probably somebody trying to bypass their water allocation meter."

"Well, it's stopped now," Jay said. "Pa says we could do with some more rain."

"The screen said situation normal this morning."

"What do you want? Situation desperate, sacrifice your goldfish?" Jay chuckled. "Admin prefers to keep the populace calm."

"It doesn't work," Gem said, "not if my pa's anything to go by. He loses his calm the minute he opens his mouth."

"How are your folks?"

"All right. Same as usual."

"Gem," Jay said, "how long have we known each other?"

"We first met," Gem said precisely, "four years and five months ago."

"And I still don't know how your parents are. Oh sure, I've met them, but they were on their best behavior then."

Gem kicked the leaves in the water channel. "Pa might be living on a different planet from me. I can't do a thing right as far as he's concerned." She fell silent, thinking of Pa as she usually saw him, his back and head bent over his work line; working, working, as if the demons would get him if he stopped. He had given the credit for the Outside key, but along with it had come the impression that it was more a reward for good work than a birthday present. "Ma goes shuttling backward and forward like a satellite on elastic," Gem said. "Trying to explain each of us to the other, she says. I don't need explaining if only Pa would try to see things my way."

"Poor lady," Jay said. Gem stepped out of the water channel on the side away from him; he took a big step across and walked beside her.

"She seems to be happy, anyway," Gem said. They came to an intersection; where the streets met, the water channels converged in a round basin. At the moment it held nothing but leaves and litter. Gem waded through the rustling heap while Jay crossed over on the gray slabs that did duty for bridges.

"Shouldn't she be happy?" Jay asked.

"She wanted another baby, but we couldn't afford it unless Pa was promoted, and then Admin messaged her to say she was past the age. Pa's promotion came through a month later."

"Oh, Gem." Jay sounded unexpectedly sympathetic.

"I'd have liked a sister," Gem said.

"Not a brother?"

"What, with you around?" Gem looked back at Jay; there was an odd expression on his face. She turned back, confused. "What about you, Jay?" she asked.

"I'd like someone." He shook himself and changed the subject so obviously that Gem could almost hear the crunch. "Who are you doing your project with?"

"Ness Brenault, heaven help me."

"Oh, you'll be all right. Ness isn't everyone's pet, but she has some good ideas." He put his arm across Gem's shoulders. "And I've known her as long as I've known you, so you can trust me."

"You keep your hands to yourself," Gem said, ducking away from his arm. "And it's Ness I don't trust."

Jay only laughed. They were almost at the Delaiah house. He turned aside, waving one hand over his shoulder to Gem. He never said good-bye if he could help it.

Gem's mother came out onto the doorstep as Gem reached home. "That girl Ness Brenault called," she said.

"Did she leave a message?" Gem jumped off the street and in through the house door.

"No," her mother said to Gem's retreating back (Gem could imagine the look of distaste). "She left you a box of rubbish."

Gem turned around, her foot on the second stair up. *"Rubbish?"*

"That's what it looks like. I put it outside your room." The distaste deepened. "She said it would help with that project of yours."

"Ultra! Thanks, Ma." Gem went on her way upstairs, three at a time. As far as they could study social history when undesirable attitudes weren't always recorded in the data banks, Gem and Ness were studying it. Their project was "Protest Songs of the Nineteenth to the Twenty-First Centuries." It had been Gem's idea to collect the texts, and Ness's to try recording the music.

The box was made from the recycled waste that dissolved if you left it in the rain, but the rubbish was very particular rubbish. Gem plunged her hands into the pile of brittle paper. She had a strong feeling that they were supposed to research only what was held in the data banks; but it looked as if Ness had broken into one of the recycling stores—which she was perfectly capable of doing. She had her own ways of finding out where restricted material was stored before it was changed into the latest cardboard box.

Downstairs the door rolled open then shut again: Pa come home. Gem shuffled a few pieces of paper together, dropped them in the box again, and decided to go down. If she said hello to Pa now, she might be spared the sarcastic "Oh, you do still live here?" next time they bumped into each other on the stairs.

An hour later, after the meal, Gem ran upstairs with a sigh of relief and dragged the box of paper into her room. She sat down and began taking everything out. Sheets of paper, brown and flaking. Black-smudged halves of pictures on the backs of some pieces.

Record this before you forget which bits you wanted. Gem scrambled onto her bed so she could reach the place where the wall had to be thumped to alert the screen. A moment of panic when the password taker wouldn't respond to her voice. Repeat in a different tone. Ness was reputed to open her line by shouting obscenities. She was reputed to do all sorts of things; Jay said she put around more rumors about herself if things got too quiet.

Back to work. Slowly Gem read aloud from the brittle leaves. Once there was some music, and a frantic scrabbling search for the mini mouse (under the pillow, of all places) to select music notation.

The papers had been so roughly heaped into the box that there seemed to be more of them than there were; Gem was through the pile in a couple of hours. The last piece in the box was a particularly good one. Gem dealt with it carefully and turned it over to see whether there was anything on the back.

More gray pictures. The words caught Gem's eye, and she read them carefully, silently. Then she messaged Ness.

"Gem here. Thanks for the—box."

"Thanks nothing. I had to get rid of it," Ness said. "Do me a favor and feed it to recycling. Was it any good?"

"Didn't you look at it?"

"Not beyond sorting it out, no."

"There was some good stuff," Gem said. "Do you want any of it?"

"Me? You're the print maniac. Just send me the music, like we said."

Gem said something vague about yes, she'd do that. She looked down at that last piece of paper. "Ness . . ."

"What now?"

"Oh, nothing." Gem said good-bye, closed the line, and ran her finger along the edge of the paper. It bent and cracked, and a flake of it drifted to the floor. The picture was dimmer than ever—with a little shock of surprise Gem realized that it was completely dark outside. She asked the computer to turn the lights on. There was a brief hum as they warmed up, and a bleep as they reached the intensity Gem liked them set to.

Gem read the back of the paper again and tried to put certain words up on the screen with the voice type. The screen did not recognize them. "Word line," Gem said, by which she meant the data-bank dictionary. Then she spoke the words aloud again. There they were: "now figurative use only"; "now figurative use only"; "obsolete"; "word not found."

Suddenly Gem felt very tired. She closed the word line but left the words and definitions so that they would come on screen when she next alerted it. With a word she canceled the lights, undressed, and rolled into bed. The words glowed for a little while in the dark, and slowly faded.

Blind. Deaf. Disabled. Wheelchair.

Maps and Secrets

Gem woke up in the morning feeling as if she had had an important dream in the night and forgotten it. The sun was shining in through the window; she had forgotten to switch the liquid crystal the night before, and the glass was still clear. She dredged up the password from the early-morning sleepiness of her brain and saw last night's words appear on the screen. They seemed to watch her as she scrambled into her clothes: strange words, from a foreign country, whose meaning nudged at the back of her mind like something forgotten, something important.

She ordered up breakfast from the dispenser. It was still very early; nobody moving in the house or outside among the grayish-white repeating planes and angles of the houses. Over in the distance a wisp of green was waving, so there must be a wind; and someone was rich enough to buy a piece of land for something as frivolous and unproductive (inside the City) as a tree. Trees belonged Outside, in the environment. Gem leaned one knee on the windowsill and chewed bread.

A whistle from the street outside; Gem looked down. "Jay! What are you doing?"

"Just passing. Can I come in?"

"I'll run down and open up, half a second."

When they were both comfortable in her room, Gem said, "Funny time of day to be just passing."

"I was up early," Jay said, stirring the papers in Ness's box with long, brown fingers. "What are these?"

"Ness gave them to me for the project." Gem looked narrowly at Jay's face. There were lines under his eyes, and his clothes were creased, as if he had been sleeping in them. He looked more as if he had been up all night than up early; and that yellowish dust on his shoes came from no City street, surely?

Gem realized that Jay was looking at her with raised brows, but before she could think of anything to say, his gaze slid behind her to the screen on the wall. He blinked, twice, and then said, "What have you been reading, Gem?"

"This." She handed him the piece of paper from on

top of the box. "The other side," she said. "I must put this down the recycler—Ness asked me to. I guess we shouldn't have seen it."

"Better put it down one of the public chutes in that case," Jay said absently, still reading. "They'll only want to know where you got it."

"Jay—do you know what they mean—those words?"

Jay looked at her over the top of the paper. Then he said, "Would you like to come Outside again this afternoon?"

Gem shut her mouth and swallowed, wishing Jay wouldn't change the subject quite so drastically; but at least it was plain that he wasn't going to answer the question. "Maybe," she said.

"If you still haven't got a key, have one of mine."

"Buying my company?" Gem snapped, and was half frightened as soon as she'd said it, partly at her own anger, partly at how Jay might take it. Is Jay that arrogant, or do I just think he is, because he's got big credit? But if he does think he can buy me—

"I didn't mean it like that," Jay said. "Do come, Gem. Call it a late birthday present, or something."

Her anger went as fast as it had come. "I've still got the one Pa gave me credit for, somewhere. Call yesterday's one the present, if you like." She stood up. "I left mine on the bed."

"Is that it? On the floor?"

"Thanks. This afternoon, you said?"

Jay nodded and said, "Time I was home." Gem came down with him to open the door, laying her hand flat on the key plate. Jay went out, flipped half a wave at her, and was gone.

Later, when she came to take the box of paper down to the public chute, Gem looked for that last piece, because she wanted to keep it; but it was nowhere to be found. Shrugging, Gem carried the box away and, when she came back, blotted the accusing words from the screen with some course work on plane geometry and computer graphics.

The afternoon was bright and shining as she waited for Jay by the City Edge gate. The light in the pale-gray streets was glaring, almost painful; it was a relief when Jay arrived and they went Outside into the wide expanse of green. The City glittered in the sun, the solar cells doing their job on every rooftop.

"Let's go around the scarp, where the river comes out," said Jay.

"Wouldn't it be quicker to cut through the City and go out the other side?"

"There isn't another gate. Come on, Gem."

They began to run, first along by City Edge, then faster and faster down the slope, west outside the City.

Near the bottom Gem caught her feet in the long grass, fell, and rolled over. The hill on which the City was built hung above her like a breaking wave.

"Hurt yourself?" Jay asked, dropping down beside her.

"No. But I have a stitch in my side." Gem lay getting her breath back, the sky crisscrossed by grass stems in front of her eyes.

"Do you think they'd let me dig up a patch?" she said. "I could grow some in my room."

"Easier to hide the seeds," Jay said, so they hunted through the grass until Gem had a handful of seeds in her pocket.

Jay got up on his knees and pushed his black hair out of his eyes. "Let's go down to the water." They waded through the grass. It was never cut here, and Gem's feet were soon tangled in yellow ropes of hay. Ahead of her Jay walked with his shoulders hunched and his hands crammed into his pockets.

Soon the grass was shorter and harsher, and Gem could see sand among the roots. And then—the river. Gem stood staring. "But—"

"But what?"

"It's much bigger when it comes out here than when it goes in. On the other side."

"Yes." Jay was being either dense or else deliberately uninformative.

Gem looked at him. "Well, why?"

"Underground springs, maybe." When she looked at him again, he smiled.

"You're not being very helpful, are you?" Gem said, and then, "Oh, never mind." She sat down and ran a handful of sand between her fingers.

"I don't," Jay said dryly, but he stood there, gazing upstream where the water came out of the scarp, looking as if he did mind very much indeed about something. Gem turned away and watched the reflected clouds dancing on the water. Then she saw the other flower. This one was white; not trumpet shaped but bowl shaped, like the water lily in the garden pond at Jay's house. Gem scrambled to her feet and darted forward. She was only ankle deep in the water when the flower drifted into her hands.

It wasn't a flower at all, but an intricately folded piece of paper. Gem lifted it out of the water. "Look, Jay!"

"I can see it," Jay said quietly.

Gem touched it. "It's dry on top."

Jay moved uneasily away from the water. "Leave it, Gem."

"No, but look, Jay, if anyone had floated it on the other side like you did, it would be soaked. If it floated at all after the drop under City Bridge."

"Shouldn't think so hard," Jay said. "Bad for the brains."

Gem opened her mouth, shut it with a snap, and said, "Oh no you don't." So Jay was trying to get her off the subject. Why? What did he know? We're friends, heaven help us, Gem thought. Or he acts as if we are, so why doesn't he trust me? I know all about him—and there Gem stopped. True, she knew his likes and dislikes, and a good deal of how he passed his time: but he never told her what he thought or dreamed of.

Jay said nothing. He was looking at the ground between his feet as if there was something he could read in the sand.

"If you don't want to talk about it, don't," Gem said at last. "But if you do have anything to say, I wish you'd say it." Jay didn't move. Gem could have shaken him. Anything to get a reaction out of him.

"Gem"—he tapped the flower—"drop that in the shredder and forget you ever saw it."

"No," Gem said. "I want to keep it."

Reaction at last: Jay grabbed her arm. "Don't tell anyone where you found it. *Don't.*"

"Whyever not?" Gem lifted the flower to her face and inspected it more closely.

Jay shook her, hard. Gem pulled away, but he held on. "Would 'Because I asked you' be a good-enough reason?" he said. "Please. Seriously."

And when was Jay ever serious? Gem looked at his face over the paper petals. "Really really seriously?" Her pulse bounced under the grip of his fingers.

"Really to the power of n seriously."

"I promise, then."

Jay let go of her. He crammed his hand down into his pocket—so that she couldn't see it was shaking, perhaps?—and turned away. "Jay," Gem said, "what's the matter?"

"Nothing."

Tentatively, she came closer. "There must be something. Or else give me a reason."

"I can't," Jay said, still with his back to her. "Please stop asking me about it."

That was twice in five minutes he'd said please. This must be serious. "All right," Gem said. "Change the subject."

"Where shall we go now?" But the bloom had gone off the afternoon; all Gem wanted to do was get back into the City and forget about secrets. She trudged upslope to the gate and, when she looked down from the Edge, saw Jay standing tall and hunched by the water. With a sigh she pushed her key through the gate and entered the City.

She spent the rest of the afternoon planting the grass

seeds in a small ceramic pot full of earth stolen from Ma's precious vegetable patch, and the evening back in the twenty-first century with songs and politics.

Next morning she treated herself to a ramble through the data banks. Not looking for anything in particular, just on the lookout for anything unusual. She did consider hacking into something more exciting, but it was so easy to get caught. And Gem knew she wasn't like Ness Brenault, who could keep two steps ahead of all Admin's detectors and come out with information that would make your hair curl: how to double your alcohol allocation; which of Admin's top officials had spent the night in whose bugged bedroom; even what the price of real meat was going to be next week if you wanted to buy it officially from the Store.

So what do I do? Gem thought. Let's have a look at that river, and see what happens to it under the City. Nothing, I expect. It probably runs straight through. But where can that paper flower have come from? "Call up map, City, combine." There's the map. "Add river."

The blue streak for the river out of the scarp glowed on the wall. They're taking this very literally. "Call up stream." Another blue streak, narrower, by City Bridge. Nothing, apparently, under the City. "Any other water."

Oh help—I didn't want the pipes. "Cut system pipes, move up, hold." Still nothing.

So what now . . . ? "City history, maps, water, nonsystem." The wall bleeped.

Map file outdated, still required?

"Yes." And there it was: a map with the river. "Take water, move up, merge scale." That should overlay the two maps onto each other.

Gem leaned forward, biting her lower lip, then put her hands to her mouth as if to hold words in.

Under the neat repeating pattern of the City streets and buildings lay a web of water like a thread unraveling and raveling again. Its two ends overlay the river on the modern map, but under all the houses, how deep it did not say, there were caves and tunnels. Large caves too, from the size of some of the blue areas. Gem's hand hovered over the wall slot where the printer was hidden. At last she whispered, "Print large please." No response. She had to say it again, louder, before the sheet of paper was spat out onto the floor.

I need a drink. What's in the dispenser?

She got down on the floor beside the printed map and weighted it down with the drink on one side and a lump of white quartz Pa had brought back from City Two on the other. A closer look showed her that two of the underground lines of water seemed to start from nowhere, just inside City Edge. Gem scrambled to her feet again and said, "Delete all not water." The blue web hung on the wall.

Once, Ness had told Jay one of Admin's confidential key sequences that let you check for interference with a file—and Jay had told Gem. She pulled the board out of the wall and looked around. I suppose someone might be watching, though where from? She darted away from the wall to dim the window, came back, and held down the key sequence.

Two red marks over where those lines started.

Data erased, refer Admin.

Ness always said Admin tampered with the data, and I didn't believe her. But they do—if this is Admin. But who else? She banged the board into the wall. "Hold for next session, cut line." The screen went blank.

Another ten minutes on her knees staring at the printed map. Gem opened line again and called up the screen.

The river map had disappeared. She couldn't re-create it using the original chain of words. Quietly, hurriedly, Gem used Ness's trick again. The screen told her:

Previous access unauthorized, alert.

"Oh *help!* Clear memory, this and previous session. Cut line and close." Gem sat still, breathing as if she had been running. Call Jay. No reply. Who else knows about the data banks?

Slowly, half against her will, Gem opened line to Ness Brenault.

"Ness? Gem Rannesen."

Ness, on the other end of the screen, half closed her green eyes. "And to what does this mere mortal owe such an honor?"

Yes, Gem thought, you know I don't like you. Well, you're going to enjoy this. "I was working on a file," she said. "Admin deleted it. What do I do now?"

"Whee-oo," Ness said. "You pray, is what. Or have you just lost it?"

"I tried that trick you told Jay."

Ness laughed out loud, tipping her head back so that her red curls swung dramatically. "Gem the prim and proper takes the first step on her life of crime."

"You shut up and tell me what I do!"

"Don't snap at me, Rannesen," Ness said coolly. "If Admin thinks you've seen something you shouldn't have, they'll be calling on you."

"But if access was unauthorized, how come they let me in anyway?"

Ness grinned. "Oh, they're not completely infallible. Destroy the evidence, if there is any." And she cut line.

Gem swung around on her chair. She'd never get the

map back if she shredded it now. . . . Carefully she folded it small, pressing as hard as she could to make it flat and smooth.

Downstairs someone knocked at the door. Gem ran to the window. Green uniforms—Admin—she whirled away from the window, clutching the map. They'll come upstairs. Where shall I hide it? She slipped the map into the waistband of her trousers and pulled her shirt out over it. Don't bend or you'll crackle. She dashed across to the chair, kicked her drink over, mopped it up with a blank sheet out of the printer, and sent that down the shredder. Orange-flavored paper next week.

She was still sitting on the floor when they knocked. "Come in!" Did she really sound that nervous?

There were two of them: one middle-aged, one young. Both looked friendly; Gem tried a smile.

"Morning," the middle-aged one said. "You been having trouble with your screen?"

"Oh no," Gem said. "Why?"

"Just a little bit of bother up at Admin," he said. "You're doing a history project, aren't you?"

"Social history," Gem said.

"Ah. Maybe hunting 'round for old material?"

"Sort of." Gem took a deep breath and said, "Ness Brenault's my project partner."

The man seemed to relax. "I see. Ness Brenault . . . maybe that explains it."

The blood was tingling in Gem's fingers, the quick of her fingernails almost hurt with it. Please let them go away. Please.

"Find anything interesting?" he said.

Don't hesitate—they'll think you're making up a story. "There was a map," Gem said, "but I couldn't work it out. Anyway, I spilled orange juice on it, so I put it in the shredder." There was the damp sticky patch on the floor to corroborate the story; she saw them both glance at it.

"Nice room," the older man said, and strolled across to the shelf where the folded paper flower lay in full view. Gem wondered if her face looked as stiff as it felt.

"Very pretty." He picked it up. "You make it?"

"No, I found it."

"Rather a waste of paper," the younger man suggested.

Gem tried her best smile on him. "Oh, I don't think it's wasted if it's beautiful."

"Studying philosophy too?" The older man chuckled and dropped the paper flower on the bed. Gem caught sight of the younger one surreptitiously straightening his collar and slicking back his hair. Perhaps another smile?

"I don't think there's anything we need to talk to you

about," said the older one. "But let's not have any more trouble, hmm?"

"Oh no," Gem said, and smiled again. When the door closed, she gritted her teeth and counted to one hundred. The street door closed, her mother switched on the music line, and Gem heaved a sigh of relief.

What now? Of all things she wanted to talk with Jay, or at least leave the map for him to look at. Only maybe—Gem pulled her jacket on and fastened the map into an inside pocket—if Admin was really suspicious, it would be waiting to see where she went.

Gem ran downstairs and into the street, her throat tight and her heart thumping. This was how she felt when she was waiting for something wonderful to happen. But now . . .

She felt as if the map must be bleeping, or glowing, on some wavelength that she could neither see nor hear. She had to fight to keep her hands down by her side, to stop them from patting the crackly rectangular patch where the map lay hidden.

Don't go too fast. Stroll. Saunter. You call at Jay's often enough; they'll think it's peculiar if you run now. Act carefree! With a wild giggle Gem jumped down into the water channel and hopscotched along it.

When Gem put her hand on the Delaiah key plate, the message box began to say, "No reply," but was interrupted by a bleep and a recorded message from Jay. "Gem, I'm not here, but if you want to wait, you can let yourself in by using your screen password. Same for my room. Carry on."

This was new. They must have connected their key plate and its handprint sensors to the main system. Well, did she want to go in if Jay wasn't there? Maybe he'd be back soon; she might as well sit in his room and wait. Gem said her password. Into the house, and the door slid shut behind her. Along the passage and down to Jay's room in the basement as quietly as if she were a burglar. Another key plate, same password. She closed Jay's door firmly and sat down on the bed to look around. A shadow crossed the room—someone passing the skylight set in the angle between the wall and the sidewalk. So odd that she could see them and they couldn't see her.

Jay was mostly on the creative-arts side. On a shelf there were a couple of small wire sculptures based on 3-D computer-graphic patterns. A panel in the wall was covered with a landscape at the moment; he painted it over and started again once a month on average.

The wall panel was standing askew, yet Gem had always thought it was built into the wall. She went to put it straight, and nearly knocked it clean over in her surprise.

Behind the panel there was an open door in the wall; a low door, just big enough to crawl through. Gem pushed the panel aside and got down onto the floor. Beyond the doorway was a tunnel, leading down into the dark. Gem took one look over her shoulder at the empty room, ducked down, and crawled forward.

3
The Tunnel

The sides of the tunnel were lined with a smooth framework—Gem couldn't think what it could be made of. Her tentative fingers touched solid earth between the bars. The floor was damp—she could feel it through the knees of her trousers.

Suppose the ceiling fell in? Gem swallowed down her panic, crawled a little farther, and reached up above her head. She touched nothing but dark. Cautiously, still with her arm raised, she stood up. Her fingers touched cold stone, centimeters above her head.

A little farther on. There was room enough for her to stand, and to swing her arms. The ground was smooth. The thudding noise was nothing but her own heart. Jay must come down here . . . it must be safe. In the pitch black it wasn't easy to keep her balance. Gem began to shuffle forward, feeling as if the dark were swirling around her.

Perhaps if she moved more confidently, she'd stop feeling dizzy. Gem tried a fine swinging pace, picking her feet up in case the ground grew rougher. She knew she couldn't be moving very fast, but with no sight to measure her progress by, it seemed as if she were rushing down into the blackness with the wind in her face.

Gem stopped short. The wind *was* in her face. She swung her arms and touched nothing. There must be space all around her, or openings in the tunnel; otherwise there would be no wind. More tunnels? She had a vision of a dark network all around her like a spider's web.

If I turn back? Which way is back? Careful steps forward, arms swinging. Stone at her fingertips. What now? If Jay comes down here, he must come back; unless I've already passed the tunnel he uses. There might be any number of tunnels. Perhaps if I keep the wind at my back?

Slowly, Gem turned around and set her back to the tunnel wall. She took four careful paces and stood waiting to feel the wind blow in her face.

Click, and a blinding light in her eyes. Gem yelped, and flung one arm across her face. Another click and the darkness came back. She blinked through the green fog of the afterimage. How tight her chest felt—her heart banging as though trying to escape. "Who—" she licked her dry lips and tried again. "Who's there?"

"Nobody you know," a girl said. "Why did you come down here?"

"Why shouldn't I?"

"Why not, indeed . . ." somebody else, a boy, murmured.

And the girl said, "All right then, how did you come down here? Who let you in?"

"I found—" Gem swallowed. This was worse than Admin. "The door was open."

"How very convenient," the girl said, and then there was silence. Gem began to wonder if they had moved away. Surely she would have heard them go?

"I was trying to find the way out," she said.

"Aren't we all?" A new voice, someone else. A brief mutter of agreement—from how many people? And who were they?

Gem took a step back. "You can't live down here."

"But we do."

It didn't seem possible. "Always? In the dark?"

"Most of the time," the girl said. "That is to say, always here, mostly in the dark." The flashlight flicked on again, the blot of light moving swiftly across faces. Four, five—how many?

"Who *are* you?" Gem said.

A boy answered, "We call ourselves the Waterbound, but you won't have heard of us."

"I haven't," Gem said. Could these be City people? In that brief glimpse she hadn't recognized any of the faces. And did Admin know? "What do you mean, Waterbound?"

"You should know your language," the girl said. "Bind, band, bound. As in binding oath, band of hope, bounden duty, homeward bound, housebound. Going somewhere, stopped from going somewhere. Us."

"I still don't understand." Gem flexed her hands nervously and clenched them together. "Can you take me back?"

"No." Another of those terrifying silences. "Where is this open door of yours?"

Maybe they didn't know that Jay came down here. Was she going to get him into trouble? Cautiously Gem replied, "In my friend's room."

There was an exasperated sigh out of the darkness. "I daresay," the girl retorted, "but which friend?"

"Jay—Jay Delaiah."

"I'll murder that boy . . . where's he gone, Mike?"

"Greenhouse, I think," said one of the boys. "You, whatsname—"

"Gem."

"Gem, then. How many people know you're down here?"

"Only you."

A grunt. "I don't suppose you shut Jay's room door behind you."

"I did! It's only coded for Jay. And me," Gem said, remembering.

"Some signs of sense," he muttered. "You want Jay, Sophie?"

"Please."

"I'll go get him," Mike said. "What about—"

"Ssh," the girl called Sophie said. "Jay will do to start with."

"I wish I could see you," Gem said.

"Do you need to?"

"It would help, maybe. You sound—short."

"I'm sitting down," Sophie said in particularly cool tones. "Have you gone, Mike?"

"You'd hardly expect me to say yes to that, would you?" Mike answered. "Anyone want taking back, since I'm going?"

"I'll come with you," someone said. "I should be with Strand Five, but Robin talked me into coming over." Two voices, one set of footsteps, moved away. There were faint noises that Gem could not identify, and a distant burst of laughter. Try as she might, she could see nothing. It was thick dark, like velvet, but not soft or warm. A cold, bitter blackness, like gall. Gem's teeth began to chatter; she wrapped her arms around herself. In the group in front of her, people were talking softly.

At last, in the distance a dot of light wavered across her vision like an errant firefly.

"Oh, come on, Jay," Sophie said under her breath. "You can manage without that."

The light came up to them. Jay was behind it, and someone else behind him. "Hello, Gem," he said.

"Hello." Gem rubbed her hands up and down her arms. "You left your hole in the wall open."

"So I gather." Jay sounded faintly amused. Did he mean to? Gem thought. Is that why he had the key plates set for me? She heard the dust grit under Jay's feet. "Will it be all right, Sophie?" he asked.

"If you vouch for her, yes as far as I'm concerned. But I'll have to ask them in the other strands." Sophie was quiet for a moment, and then sighed. "Jay," she said, "she has not the faintest idea what all this is. You had better tell her."

Gem could still see only the outlines of people, a flick of movement shining on skin and hair. Jay was keeping the flashlight pointed at the floor. He said, "Talk among yourselves for a moment, then."

The murmur of conversation rose again. Jay pulled Gem aside and bent down so that his mouth was by her ear. She felt his breath on her neck.

"Gem," he muttered, "if you make one movement to look as if you're frightened or—or as if you don't like it—I'll never speak to you again. Never."

The darkness seemed to grow huge and threatening above them. Was Jay waiting for her to answer? Gem clenched her hands together.

"You hear me?" Jay said.

"Yes." Gem shivered.

"Good." Jay dimmed the flashlight and flicked it to wide beam. "Gem," he said, "I want you to meet my friends."

The light showed a tall girl with pale-ginger hair and green eyes. "This is Sal," Jay said. "She's deaf."

"Deaf?"

"She can't hear."

She looks normal, Gem thought. Is that what it looks like to be deaf? "Robin, in the wheelchair." The flashlight swung down beside Jay. Robin was sitting down. The wheelchair looked as if it had been welded in odd places and then lashed together with wire. Robin had no legs. Gem's heart started another escape bid. Bang bang bang, get me out of here. "Hi there, Gem," Robin said, grinning. He was dark, good-looking. Gem pushed her mouth into a smile. "Theo," Jay went on. An angular face with black eyebrows that almost met above the bridge of his nose, and a crooked smile. Jay said, "Theo shares life with what used to be called cerebral palsy when these things were all open and above ground. Mike—" the light swung to an oval face under a lot of fair hair, "you've heard already. He's blind—what the word line would call 'unable to see.' And finally, for the moment, Sophie."

Sophie was sitting in another wheelchair, in front of Sal. She looked at Gem expressionlessly: no smile, no greeting. She had black hair past her shoulders, and her face was so thin that all the bones showed clearly. Jay narrowed the beam so that the light was on her only above the waist.

"Any questions?" Sophie said.

Gem moved a little nearer to Jay. "I'll ask Jay later."

"How tactful." A faint smile glimmered on Sophie's face. "I must go and clear you with the others."

Robin said, "I pulled the plug on the glowworms when Mike scouted in with the news, so I'd better fix them now."

Gem wondered what he meant—it was like a different language. She wondered if she had looked as startled as she felt. Had she, maybe, looked frightened? Not by the people, the thought scurried through her head, but by the impossibility of it. The words from that missing piece of newsprint that had glared at her from her screen; out of the obsolescence, the nonexistence that the word line had given them, they had come to her in this place under the City. They were here, real, after all.

Sophie reached up and back, and tapped Sal's hand. Sal moved around to face her, so that her back was to Gem, and all she could see was a movement of hands. Presently Robin joined in. It seemed as if the gestures had form and pattern, but she could not understand them.

"Right," Robin said, "that's settled. Sal takes Sophie to the other strands and Jay and whosit come with me."

"Her name's Gem," Jay said.

Robin flashed another grin at Gem. "I remember your name, of course," he said, "but we all like getting a rise out of Jay." He spun the chair around. "You come in front with the light, Jay."

It seemed a long walk. They passed through a wide cave where Jay flung the light into the corners to show makeshift beds: a pad of cloth for a pillow, much-patched blankets. The floor was smooth, worn and darkened as if many people had passed up and down along the years. Through openings in the cave side Gem heard a distant sound of voices. How many people could there be down here?

"Robin's wonderful workshop will now fix the glowworms," Robin said, and turned aside into one of the tunnels.

Gem had visions of luminous insects. "Glowworms?" she said. A line of dim lights appeared along the roof.

Jay switched the flashlight off and said, "Glowworms."

"What are they?"

"Old-fashioned vacuum bulbs," Jay said. "Connected by wires. See Admin's *Basic History of Technology*, screen forty-three."

Gem sat down on the ledge cut out of the wall, shivering. "I never knew, never guessed there was such a place down here."

"So far as I know," Jay said, "you're the fourth person from Upstream who knows. Perhaps a very few others, but if so they're keeping it to themselves." He sat down beside her and rested his clasped hands on his knees. "Upstream," he said again, as if it had a capital letter.

"Who are the other three?" The lights dimmed briefly and recovered.

Jay's face flickered as he said, "Me; Kate Avrassian, from Childcare, at the hospital; and Bill, her partner. Kate comes if anyone needs medical help, and Bill if the Waterbound are desperate for technical help. He works for Admin, in the recycling sector."

"And why do you come down?" Gem asked.

Jay opened his mouth and shut it again. He looked at

Gem, then stood up and almost ran across to one of the openings in the rock wall. "Mike!" Gem heard him call, and then, "Is Mike back?" A brief, inaudible discussion, then Jay turned back and said, "Robin needs the flashlight. I want to take you somewhere, but it'll be dark. Can you manage?"

"Of course," Gem said.

"It's through here." Jay took hold of her hand without waiting to ask, and set off at a fast pace. Gem was almost glad she had to concentrate so much on keeping her feet: It meant she needn't think about anything else. In the dark more ways than one: uncertain, feeling her way, a little frightened. The tunnel seemed to go on forever.

They turned another corner, and suddenly Gem could see. Light shone on the walls of the tunnel, the white light of a fine day. Around another bend, and there was a long glass window, almost hidden by plants. It was warm like a greenhouse; outside, the sky was blue. Gem walked straight up to the window.

"It doesn't open," Jay said. It didn't even give a good view, being set deep between two banks of grass-grown earth, but it let in plenty of light. Straight up the view was clear: sky, a few clouds.

"Where are we?" Gem asked.

"Outside City Edge. In one of the forbidden zones."

"Who are these people? Why do they live here?"

"I can't tell you that," Jay said. "Not unless the others decide I can."

"You mean that girl in the chair?"

"Sophie," Jay said, quite fiercely for him. "She is Sophie. Just you remember that. Yes, she and the speakers for the other strands. There's more than one group down here, I can tell you that much. People grown up, grown old, some of them with children. More than a hundred all together, Sophie says."

"But *why*?" Gem demanded. "Why?"

"Don't be in such a hurry," Jay replied. "You won't like it."

Someone behind Gem spoke, in a voice so like Jay's that Gem was startled. "Were you looking for me, Jay?"

"I want you to meet Gem. She found the way down from my room."

Gem turned around. Jay moved to stand next to the newcomer. Someone a little shorter, thinner than Jay, but the same dark skin and hair. Almost, but not quite, the same face.

"Gem," Jay said, "I want you to meet my brother."

"But—" Gem shook her head, and sat down where she was. "I give up."

"You were going to say?" Jay said, sitting down himself, and resting his hands on his crossed ankles.

"I was going to say you haven't got a brother, but since

you obviously have, there's no point." Gem swallowed suddenly. She had noticed that Jay's brother seemed to keep one arm hidden behind his back, but when he sat down she saw that in fact he had only one arm.

After a moment the stranger said, "I have a face too. You can look at that if you like."

Gem could feel herself blushing. She looked desperately at Jay. He wasn't going to help; he looked the other way. His brother held out his hand. "Shake. Any friend of Jay's, you know. And it won't come off."

Gem laughed nervously and took the offered hand. "Hi, I'm Gem Rannesen."

"And I'm Jon Delaiah, commonly called J2 by this lazy creature here."

Jay chuckled, and Jon added, "Unfortunately it caught on, and now all the Waterbound call me J2—when I have a perfectly good name of my own."

"I don't think you two are going to bite each other," Jay said, getting to his feet, "so I'll leave you to it. Is Mel still down here, J2?"

"She may be. Try the other end."

Jay strolled away. Gem couldn't think what to say next. However hard she tried, she couldn't help looking at the few centimeters of J2's left arm, then glancing at his face to see if he'd noticed, then looking away again in case he had.

"Look at it if you like," J2 said. "And you're obviously bursting with unasked questions."

Gem blushed again. "Does it hurt?"

"Not for any reason other than your own would."

She managed half a laugh. "Stupid question."

"Maybe." He grinned at her, his eyes crinkling. "Next?"

"What happened to it?"

"I was born is what happened to it. It came with me."

Gem twiddled a lock of her hair around her fingers. "Jay says he can't tell me why you're all down here."

J2 said, "If you mean by that, will I, the answer is no, not exactly. But you've been introduced to enough of us—you ought to be able to work it out for yourself." He leaned back against the glass, wriggling his shoulders. Then he tipped his head back and relaxed all over like a sunbathing cat.

"What time is it?" Gem asked.

"About two in the afternoon by the look of the sun."

Two in the afternoon! Gem swallowed. She hadn't even had time to tell Jay about the map and Admin, so much had happened, and it was still the same day. "Does Jay come down here much?" she asked.

J2 opened his eyes a very little and looked more than ever like a sleepy cat. "Oh yes. He's the only one who comes Downstream at all often."

Gem turned her back to the window. The pool of light stretched beyond the plants, then dried into darkness. There were other people; when she looked along the wall of glass, she saw them, sitting in the sun as J2 was doing, some apparently reading, or with their heads down over work. One boy, whose back was to her, twitched and jerked continuously as if invisible wires were being pulled. There was a girl with fair hair who had no arms. Someone with a round face was laughing, at nothing Gem could see. Other people. The differences leaped at her wherever she looked.

"J2," she said, "there was a word I saw. On some old newsprint."

"Yes?"

"Disabled."

"That's the one."

"Is everyone here—Downstream—are they all—?" She couldn't go on.

"Yes, they are."

Gem sat still, not saying anything but not feeling quiet. Why had she never seen anything like this in the City? The answer came with the precision of an elegant equation: Because they are all down here.

"If you don't like it," J2 said, "you had better go now."

"I never knew anything about this; how can I know if I like it?" Gem suddenly felt like banging her fists on her head. "I just never knew, and I don't understand. Why doesn't Jay come back?"

"He'll be talking to Mel," J2 said. "Melanie Talmann."

"But I used to know the Talmanns!" Gem said, amazement making her voice squeak. "They lived next door for ages."

"Yes, Jay told me."

"But do they know about Mel?"

"Not one of the things I can tell you," J2 said. "Look, here they come. Be tactful and don't ask her about it, hmm?"

Jay and Mel arrived together, holding hands. Mel had a perfect pink-and-white complexion and light-brown curly hair. She let go of Jay's hand when they stopped walking and looked around uncertainly.

"Hello, Mel," J2 said. "Sit down?" He reached up his hand. Mel took it and sat with her head bowed, making odd movements with her hands and fingers.

Jay said, "Mel, I brought you some more paper." He reached inside his jacket and held out a handful of paper squares. Mel looked up, blue eyes wide open. "For me?" she whispered.

"For you," Jay agreed, and put the paper into Mel's lap. Her hands began to move again around one of the squares, folding and unfolding almost too fast for Gem to see what she was doing. At last Mel held up her hand. On her palm lay a paper flower, twin to the one Gem had taken out of the river yesterday.

"It's beautiful!" Gem said.

"Show Gem how, Mel," said Jay.

Mel smiled and gave one of the squares to Gem. She took another herself, folded it once, and took Gem's hands in hers to repeat the movement. One by one the folds and creases, until Gem could do the last petal by herself. Two more lilies floated on the dusty floor.

"How did you learn this, Mel?" Gem asked.

"A book," Mel said, almost inaudibly.

Gem twirled the lily she had folded, so that it spun jerkily in the dust. "I found one of these in the river," she said. A tug at her sleeve. Was Jay trying to attract her attention? "It came floating out into the sunshine, and I thought it was lovely."

"There's no out," Mel said. "Only in." She got up and walked away into the dark.

The Hollow World

4

There was silence by the window. J2 got to his feet, said, "I'll go and see she's all right," and followed after Mel.

"She isn't, of course," Jay said. "You shouldn't talk to Mel about Upstream, Gem."

"How was I to know?"

"You weren't." Jay looked up at Gem. "If you came to my room, I suppose you wanted to see me about something, but why couldn't you leave a message on the screen?"

Gem said, "What else could I do when I found the door?"

The folded map was burning in her pocket. Halfway to reaching for it, she said, "Jay, did you mean me to come down here? Fixing your key plates for me, leaving the tunnel open?"

Jay's face went blank with surprise. "No. Were you thinking that?"

"Sort of. Would you rather I hadn't come?"

"Sort of," Jay answered, half mocking.

I wish I knew what he thinks of me, Gem thought. Am I just a flaming nuisance?

And then Jay added, "All the same, I am glad you've found out. It's going to be a change, to be able to talk about it. But don't—repeat don't—expect me to talk about it indoors."

"What are you frightened of?" Gem said. "Bugs in the walls?"

"Yes," said Jay simply.

Gem swallowed, took a deep breath, and said, "Two men from Admin came around to my room this morning."

"*What?*" said Jay. "Gem, what have you been doing?"

Gem looked at him to see if he was laughing at her. To her surprise she saw a look of acute anxiety on his face. Slowly she reached inside her jacket and took out the folded map.

"I was . . . just trawling through the data bank," she said. "Looking for maps, wondering about the river."

"There are no maps of the river," Jay said.

"You can't have looked hard enough. I found this one."

Jay snatched it out of her hands and began unfolding it frantically. "Gem, you're a marvel," he said, and then stopped and stared. "Was this what brought Admin around? What did you tell them?"

"I told them it was down the shredder. I don't know whether they believed me."

"They'll act as if they didn't," said Jay, still unfolding. "Just to make sure. So you had to come straight to me?"

"I wanted your advice!" Gem looked at Jay. He was kneeling down by the map, feverishly tracing lines with his finger. She knelt down beside him. "So where are we?"

His finger hovered and stabbed. "There. In one of the forbidden zones, like I said."

Gem looked. "Where that river's marked? It said 'data erased' on the main file."

Jay shot a glance at her but didn't question her knowledge. "Yes, that's why it's a forbidden zone." He stood up and looked out the window. "See that long dip in the ground? You'd see it better from City Edge. There's a river under there. The other forbidden zone's the same."

"Two rivers we're not allowed to know about?" Gem said incredulously. "And Admin always at us to save water—not to mention your pa worrying when it doesn't rain," she added, remembering.

"If there's a long enough time without rain," Jay said

dryly, "someone is going to realize that there isn't actually a drought. And you can't deny, it is better not to waste water. Anyway—the map!" He turned and knelt down again. Gem wished he would calm down.

As if he had heard her wishing, Jay sat back on his heels and put his hands to his head. "Let me *think*," he said, and was quite still while Gem could have counted to ten.

"We have to keep the map hidden," Jay said. "Down here will do. We have to keep the Waterbound hidden from Admin. You won't say anything?"

"No!"

Gem watched Jay folding up the map. "Is it really so— such a secret?" she asked. Jay looked at her. Gem lowered her gaze. All right, it was a secret.

Suddenly Jay sucked in his breath and said, "*Help*—if Admin's called on me—" He stood up in one swift movement and pulled Gem to her feet. "Come on, we must go."

"I closed your door," Gem said resentfully, rubbing her wrist where he had grabbed hold of her.

"They'll get in if they want to." Jay ran back through the line of plants, switched his flashlight on, and ran ahead with Gem behind him. They came to a doorway— a real doorway with a door—that was half open. Gem had a glimpse of a floor knee deep in what looked like crumpled paper. Mel was sitting at a high bench, J2 beside her. She was folding paper.

J2 looked up, and Jay jerked his head to beckon him out. "I'll be back soon, Mel," J2 said. Mel smiled vaguely and went on folding.

"2," Jay said in a hoarse whisper as soon as they were out of earshot, "take this." He pressed the folded map into J2's hand. "You and Sophie and the rest, put your heads together over it and see what you think. I've got to take Gem back. I'll be down again soon."

"Bring Gem," J2 said.

"Up to Sophie." Jay flashed a smile at his brother and ran off. Gem went a little way, then turned and waved. The lights were so dim that she could not see for certain whether J2 waved back. When she turned around again, the glimmer of Jay's flashlight had nearly disappeared, hidden by a bend of the tunnel. Gem buttoned her jacket and ran after him.

"Jay," she panted, "wait for me."

He slowed a little, but Gem was still too out of breath to talk to him as she toiled up the slope behind the blink of light in Jay's hand.

At last Jay opened the tunnel door and said, "After you," which seemed absurdly polite after all the shocks Gem had had that day.

"Thank you," she said, and scrambled into Jay's room.

Jay hauled himself through using just his arms, like a swimmer through a submerged window. He grabbed the painted panel, slammed it into place, and thumped the wall to alert his screen. He muttered his password so quietly that Gem didn't hear it; but the screen must have, for it opened line at once.

"Praise be," Jay said. "No calls." He collapsed backward onto the bed with a whistle of relief.

"Would Admin leave a call up?" Gem said. "Wouldn't they just come and go?"

"You're getting very wise all of a sudden," Jay said.

I suppose, Gem thought, he must take fear of Admin for granted, or something. What she said was, "I wouldn't have been so frightened if I hadn't known they had a reason for coming." Remembering, she sat down on the edge of the bed as if her knees couldn't hold her up.

"Yes . . ." Jay said. "Look, Gem, we'll talk about it properly next time we go Outside."

"I want to know now." There's only so long you can hold on with unasked, unanswered questions boiling around in your brain.

"I can't tell you now," Jay said. "This house, Pa being who he is, is bugged at regular intervals, and it's just about to start. See?"

A small red light near the screen blinked at slow intervals. "Bug detector," Jay said. "Ness fixed it for me."

"How did you persuade her to do that?" Gem asked, a little suspicious. Ness never did anything for free; even out of the kindness of her heart cost you something.

"Credit," Jay said. "She'd had another little talk with Admin, so she was even shorter of it than usual."

"I don't know why they don't just lock her up."

"They tried once. She claimed infringement of civil liberties." Jay chuckled. "Pa says they're just waiting for her to get her education points and then they'll offer her a job, big credit. She knows all the dodges—she'll catch all their hackers for them."

The red light began to flash faster; soon it was a continuous glow.

"Are you coming to Shan's party tonight?" Jay asked.

Gem's jaw dropped. "You mean you—oh, I'd completely forgotten," she said, trying to sound natural as Jay made frantic signals to keep secrets where they belonged, underground, shut off. "Is it—is it going to be a good party?"

"Strictly within the legal decibel limit, but yes," Jay said. "Shan's people always do her proud on her birthday, don't they?"

They talked group talk, the sort of thing Admin might expect to hear from two teenagers, until Gem could have screamed with the sheer irrelevance of it. Yet only the day before yesterday they had done the same, and Gem had been contented.

The red light began to flicker again, and at last vanished. Jay cut his last sentence off as if he had pressed a button, and said, "I was Downstream early. I must get some sleep before the party." He hesitated, looking oddly uncertain. "You'll be there?"

"Yes."

"You . . . don't mind?"

"About what?"

"The secrets I keep."

"No." Gem wondered why he felt the need to ask. "You can trust me, Jay. I'm not like Ness."

Jay chuckled, quite in the old way. "No—less expensive."

"But better quality," Gem retorted, and stalked off. You can't slam an automatic door, but you can make enough noise smacking your hand into the key plate.

The party was better than average, and Gem was quite enjoying it until she saw, among all the faces and the multicolored lights, the younger of the two Admin men who had come to see her that morning. He pushed, as straight as he could for dodging the intervening couples, through the dance toward her. Gem turned her back.

"Hello," he said in her ear.

"Hi." She made no move to turn around.

"I'm not in uniform," he said. "I'm human—you can talk to me."

Gem turned her face about ten degrees toward him. "Suppose I don't want to?"

"My name's Morgan," he said. "Morgan Smith."

"Hello, Morgan," Gem said, since it was so obviously what he wanted.

"I wanted to have a word with you," Morgan said, "because of something Chris was saying."

"Chris?"

"Chris Peters, my boss. This morning."

"Oh, yes," said Gem, feeling her stomach flutter.

"He was checking a few things," Morgan began. Gem had never known you could feel so lonely in the middle of a crowd. Morgan, getting no response, went on. "You've used more paper than you've recycled."

"Is that *all*?" Gem said, laying on the incredulity as thick as she could manage.

"It depends," Morgan said. "On what happened to the paper. You may have used it for that pretty flower, for example."

"I told you I found that," Gem said, and thought that, for all she knew, they might be standing right over the map at that moment. The dance floor suddenly became a teetering platform over the void, a long way above the solid earth where J2 and Mike and Sophie lived. She shut her eyes and opened them again. Morgan Smith didn't seem to have noticed anything.

"Oh yes," he said. "You found it."

"Which just goes to show," Gem said, "that anyone can lose a piece of paper, and if I have some you can't trace, then that's what happened."

"Don't sound so fierce!" he said. "I believe you."

Gem was wondering whether she believed him when he added, "I'll believe you permanently if you'll give me a kiss."

Oh yeuch, was Gem's first reaction. She looked at the pink skin and mousy hair. He'll be clammy. He'll be a problem either way—but I suppose he might be less dangerous if I do what he wants. Still—yeuch.

"All right," she said, and braced herself, trying not to be obvious.

When Ness fetched up beside her a little while later, Gem was still scrubbing her lips with the back of one hand. "My," Ness said, "the virtuous Gem Rannesen hard at it."

"Anything to get him off my back," Gem said unwisely, and received the stock response: "He'll have you on your back if you don't look out. Who is he, anyway?"

"Morgan Smith. From Admin."

"From Admin!" Ness smiled. "Just what I wanted. I think I'll see what I can do with him."

"Ness, he's horrible!"

"I'm not interested in their bodies, didn't you know?" Ness said. "All I want is to have them twisted around my little finger." She winked at Gem and made a beeline for Morgan Smith. Gem looked away, searching for Jay. He arrived not long afterward, and presently she found herself dancing with him.

"Sorry I was late," Jay said. "Overslept."

"Just when did you get up?" Gem asked, meaning, When did you go Downstream? Jay smiled, giving nothing away. "I don't know how you can come to parties and be so—so cool," Gem said. Someone might hear her, but they wouldn't know exactly what she meant.

"I've had a lot of practice," Jay said. "Twelve years." He stamped dramatically on the floor. "Dancing on the hollow world. What are you looking at?"

"You know the two men from Admin?"

"Not personally, but I perceive your meaning."

"One of them's here. Ness has just gone into a clinch with him."

Jay twisted around to look. "So she has. Should we warn him?"

"He deserves it," Gem said. Her eyes widened suddenly. "I think I just saw Ness pick his pocket."

They lost sight of that part of the hall for a while. Gem caught a brief glimpse of Ness by the music source. When Gem saw her again, Ness was linking arms with Morgan Smith.

Between one beat and the next the decibel level soared. Gem, glancing at Jay, saw him roaring with laughter. He bent down and shouted into Gem's ear, "I think that must be Ness's birthday present to Shan!"

"What do you mean!" Gem yelled back, and then, "She just unpicked his pocket!"

"She must have pinched his card—delimited the decibel level," Jay shouted. "When Admin comes storming around, it'll find this was authorized. By Ness's friend." His eyes were sparkling. "Come on, Gem, dance yourself dizzy!"

Gem came in from the party drunk—not on the tiny amount of alcohol that Admin doled out—but drunk on noise and movement. The house was dark. Gem tiptoed up to her room, dispensed herself some water, and crawled into bed. She could not sleep. The ghost of the evening's music still pounded through her brain, and the room swung in the dark as if she were still dancing. She lay flat on her back and made herself relax, suddenly remembered Morgan Smith, and rolled over. She thought of black velvet, which was her usual cure for insomnia: soft, deep-black velvet. Slowly she drifted asleep, down into the black. But it turned cold, and she wandered through dreams of long tunnels where a bitter wind blew.

5

Strand Seven

Things are different now, was the first thing Gem's brain said to her when she awoke. For a moment she couldn't remember why, and then the dreams seeped back into her memory.

She hadn't bothered to undress the night before. Remind me not to do that again. I feel all clammy. A memory of Morgan Smith's lips. I won't do that again in a hurry, either. Clean clothes, something to drink. Call Jay.

The screen bounced her call back at her:

DND on. Please record message.

"Do Not Disturb?" Gem said to the absent or oblivious Jay. "What do you call yesterday? I want to talk. Call me." An afterthought: "Please." She cut the call line and opened line to college. Work would be better than sitting brooding over breakfast.

Gem was deep in the early theory of holograms when the screen flickered and turned into a call from Ness Brenault. "A bone to pick with you, Rannesen," she said.

"How come you overrode college line?"

"Never mind that. You really dropped me in it, didn't you? Telling those Admin dims I was doing the same project as you. Fishing up maps out of nowhere for them to come and ask me about."

"What did you tell them?" Gem said, uncomfortably aware of the grip of tension around her throat and chest.

"I told them," Ness said, slowly and deliberately, "that we are studying songs. And if—*if* I say again—you had found a map, it was none of my business what you did with it."

"You didn't tell them I called you?"

"What do you take me for?" Ness snapped. "If they get you on this, they get me as well, and I'm kind of attached to my credit."

Gem took some deep breaths, making herself calm down. "Was it Morgan Smith?"

"No, it was Chris Peters." Ness smiled, showing her teeth. "I've now got his call code. This is being charged to him, can't be traced, can't be recorded."

"Unless they've bugged my room since yesterday."

"Yow—I never thought of that," Ness muttered. "I'll be right over." The visual cleared to screen eighteen of hologram theory. Gem made herself do some more work but at last gave up, yawned, and tied in to call line. Six words—no sound, no picture—sat in the center of the screen.

Come and see the garden. Jay.

The street door rumbled open. That would be Ness. Gem cut line, opened one of her wall panels, and stowed the paper flower and the planted grass seeds out of sight.

"Your ma doesn't approve of me," Ness said as she came into Gem's room. Gem shut her teeth on the retort: Neither do I. But she had to admit that Ness could be useful. "Close your eyes, Gem," she said. "If you don't see where I put it, you can't tell them."

"As if I would!"

"Oh," Ness said dryly, "you wouldn't mean to. Shut your eyes or go outside."

Gem shut her eyes. In a little while Ness said, "Watch for a red light on the screen. No harm in knowing where that is."

"I can't see anything," Gem said, opening her eyes.

"Nobody listening, is why." Ness slipped something down the front of her shirt. "Two credits cheap enough for you?"

"Sure."

"Make it one five later, then, and a glass of fresh orange juice now."

"Sure," Gem said again, and wondered bitterly just how it was Ness could pick on something she had ordered up only that morning. At least there was enough for two, but that would be the week's ration of fresh; back to synthetic tomorrow.

Ness said, diffidently, as she sipped the juice, "Wish I had a room of my own."

"Shouldn't you have one?" Gem swiped a stray trickle of orange from the outside of her glass. "There are rules." There were far too many rules, she thought. All for their own good, of course. Crowded people were unhappy people, so space apart for everyone. One day, maybe, when the environment could take it, the City would grow again. One day.

"Course there are, and course I should have one," Ness said, "but being legal comes expensive for us low-levellers. My brother's girl had triplets—didn't pay for the scan—so I get the overflow." She thumped the empty glass down and jumped to her feet. "Let me out of the house, will you?" They went downstairs together.

"Babies," Ness said forcibly, as if she'd been bottling the word up since she'd mentioned the triplets. "Mess both ends. Who wants 'em?" She jumped down the last four steps, and Gem had a sudden mental picture of her mother in the front room wincing at the noise.

When Gem came outside with her, Ness said, "Coming my way?" and managed to sound both surprised and suspicious at once.

"No," Gem said, and went to call on Jay.

The Delaiah house was built on a square plane with a garden courtyard in the middle. Jay was standing beside the miniscule fountain. The sound of running water was not much more than a rustle, a noise blending with the whisper of leaf on leaf, and the birdsong.

"Where's the bird?" Gem asked. There were plenty of birds Outside—they flew over the City—but there wasn't reason for them to stop except in gardens like Jay's. No crumbs, no waste heaps, precious little free water.

"In the sound line," Jay replied. "But we did have a real live bird here last week. It was brown." He dabbled his fingers in the water. "Coming down?"

"You mean Sophie said I could?"

"She said you may as well know everything, since you know something now." Jay spoke quietly, hardly audible above the noise of water. "Provided, of course," he added, "that we can trust you."

Gem smacked her hand down on the water and sent

bright droplets flying. "Don't you?" she demanded.

"Gem, sweetie," Jay said, "I trust your intentions. It's your enthusiasms make me nervous." He began to walk indoors.

Gem glared at him. "Jay, don't laugh at me. I have to know what's going on."

Jay turned on his heel and looked at her. She wanted to look away but couldn't. "All right," he said. "I trust you. Come on."

Inside his room Jay checked for the red light and knelt down by the panel in the wall. "There's a fingertip pad on the top edge," he said. "Programmed to unlock for my fingerprints."

"Do you usually leave it open?" Gem asked.

He shook his head. "I was careless yesterday. Usually I close it." He flicked a glance over his shoulder at the screen. "Remember I came past your place the other morning? The inner door had jammed shut." Another backward glance. No red light. "I had to go down again and up through Kate Avrassian's room in Childcare. She wasn't pleased." He picked up the panel. "Put your fingers there. I'll program you in." Hardly a moment, and it was done. Jay threw the programmer on the bed and fitted the panel into place. "Now you open it."

Gem put her hands to the wall. She could feel the

brush strokes in the paint Jay used, smooth and rough at once. Here was the fingertip pad: She pressed. The panel came away, and she pushed the inner door behind it open. A gust of cold air in their faces.

"Go on," Jay said. Gem wriggled cautiously forward and heard the noise of Jay following her, a scrape of wood or metal on the ground as he closed the door. "Don't worry," he said, "I've fixed it not to jam again."

"I hope so!" There was a click, and a pool of light on the ground in front of them. "I do actually know the way without the flashlight," Jay said as they stood up, "but I like to be able to see."

One day, Gem vowed to herself, I'll learn the way, and come here on my own. She wondered how Jay had ever found his way down here. About his tunnel. About J2. On the move, in the dark like this, didn't seem the best time to ask. "Where are we going?" she asked instead.

"Strand Seven, where we were yesterday," Jay answered. "One particular group of the Waterbound, the people our age or thereabouts. A little bit of Downstream."

Jay padded on. The flashlight glimmered on a floor of yellow dust. "If you hear someone talking about going 'Downstream beyond,'" he said, "don't ask what they mean by it."

"Why not?"

"Because you won't get an answer." Jay looked at her. "Keep your eyes on the path, Gem," he said.

Gem shrugged one shoulder and walked on. A suspicion of light, hardly enough to be called a glimmer, came from the string of vacuum bulbs at waist height along the wall; and then, farther along, a bright light shone from the doorway she had seen yesterday. Jay stopped and knocked. "Mel? It's Jay."

Mel whispered "Hello," and looked up briefly. There was a solar lamp on the table, the latest model. Paper rustled around Gem's feet. She looked down: ankle deep in paper flowers, a flood of delicate sharp folds, sibilant whisper of petal against petal. Some of the flowers were so big they had to be held in two hands, but Gem could have closed one hand over others without crushing them. They were all colors: blue, green, red, some white.

Mel seemed already to have forgotten that Gem and Jay were there, and they went out again. Through another tunnel, into another cave.

"Is that all she does?" Gem asked.

"It's how she passes her time," Jay said.

"What's wrong with her?"

"And what precisely would you call wrong?" Jay said savagely. "With her, or Sophie, or Mike? They are who

70

they are, and wrong or right is none of your business."

Gem sheered away from him, fighting down the tears of anger prickling at the backs of her eyes. How was she supposed to know what she should say?

If he noticed she was angry, Jay ignored it. They stood like two children refusing to talk to each other, back to back.

"Here's Sophie," Jay said at last, with what might have been relief in his voice. Gem turned around, expecting to find herself facing Sophie. She had forgotten about the chair, and had to look down.

Sophie was looking at her, half smiling. "An invitation from Strand Seven," she said. "Come and listen to the talk. The glowworms, as a special concession for Up-streamers, have been lit in the group room." Sophie swung the chair around, so that the wheels gritted in the dust. "Jay persuaded us to do it on the grounds that you might be coming down. Using three times our usual on you, we are, and all because he said so."

"Be fair," Jay said. "I got you the batteries."

Sophie snorted. "A few handfuls of used zinc-and-copper discs in the weakest salt solution you ever saw."

"What do you want me to do?" Jay asked. "Weep into it?" Sophie laughed out loud and wheeled herself across to an archway, beyond which Gem could hear voices. She felt suddenly nervous—more new people, staring at her, not trusting her? But Jay behind her said, "Go on, Gem," and she stepped forward.

Once, so long ago that Gem could hardly remember it, her parents had made her go to a children's party. One thing she did remember: the long moment in the doorway, then stepping in as if over the edge of a cliff. And everyone suddenly rushing forward to find out all there was to know about her.

It was not like that now. Or rather, the feeling of stepping over the edge was, but when she was in the room, silence came like raindrops in a puddle; small widening circles that spread and then faded away. Some faces turned briefly toward her, then back.

"You'd think I wasn't here," she muttered to Jay.

"Bad manners to stare when you meet new people," Jay said. "Do you want to be introduced?"

"What I really want," Gem said, nerves suddenly making her voice rise sharp and clear above the murmur of talk, "is to know how come everyone's down here."

This time the silence really came. Gem saw several people turn to face her; then they seemed to make themselves look away again.

"Well," Jay said softly, "Sophie tells it best, if willing."

Sophie, unmoving, said, "Not that willing, but I'll tell her."

Gem looked around for something to sit on, but there was only the floor. She sat on that. Jay folded up beside her and put his hand on hers. After a moment she pulled her arm away and fingered the fine dust. From this angle Sophie was a dark figure against the light from the bulbs; such a dim, unnatural light it could almost be called brown.

"In the days when it all began," Sophie said in a dry ironical voice, "which was a great while ago, they—and they weren't called Admin in those days—realized that there wasn't enough credit around for the City to run the medical service. So they held a meeting, or cast a vote, or maybe they just flipped a coin (it was that long ago, they still had coins as well as credit) to decide whether what credit there was should be spent on normal people making a normal contribution to City life, or on people who might not be able to contribute to a life that was designed against them, and who were in any case too young to be allowed to put their point of view. Perhaps I simplify"—the irony deepened—"but since they in the City were all, heaven help us, normal, guess who lost. That was the Ruling. Ever since then, babies like us officially die when they are born. The parents are told their baby can't be saved. Unofficially—if the baby is one of the lucky ones—it ends up down here."

"And before the Ruling," a boy said, his voice a little

husky in the still, cool air, "about twenty years before (it was a long slow business, so slow that nobody could be quite sure what was happening until it was too late), there was the Decision. They balked at 'disposing of' the adults who were like us." Gem remembered; this was Robin's voice. "So once upon a time, as a reward, or consolation, or maybe something else entirely, those adults were allowed to retire, and go to City Two before their time. We know this because of the story. Admin may know but has no records."

"What we don't know," Sophie said, "is whether those who were sent had any choice in the matter. They were, as far as we know, never harmed, but some of them, who maybe suspected something, chose to come back."

"They traveled by night," Robin went on, "and in winter, because they thought it might be too late come spring. Some of them died in the snow, and some—it is rumored—were picked off by what was to become Admin. But some of them found their way Downstream, here, and were in time to take care of the first babies saved from the Ruling, never mind how, by Ellen Beeston, who long ago had the job that is now Kate Avrassian's, and who is unrecorded in the world Upstream."

"And most of us owe our lives to Bethan Ellis," said Sophie. "Now there is Kate Avrassian. Before Bethan there was someone else. There's been someone, most times. Not always."

Silence fell. Gem was reminded of the literature readings her parents used to send her to, or one of the less embarrassing faith meetings. She strained her eyes around her into the dim light. It was like being in another time, another world. Jay was so still and silent that he might as well not have been there. Gem clenched her hands together; it felt like all she had to hold on to.

"But how can you just *stay* here?" she burst out. "Someone could go—Kate could say something—anything."

"There's only one of Kate, and she has a job to keep and two small children," Sophie said.

"But what about your parents? Don't they know?"

Robin said, "No. How could they keep us secret?"

"And," Sophie said, "supposing we found they didn't want us? We've got life at least. Let's make the best of it."

Gem shook her head, as if she could clear it that way. "Jay, couldn't you—?"

"I'd push the whole City through my tunnel tomorrow if I thought it would make any difference."

"Wouldn't it?"

"Who'd come, who'd care?" Jay said. "Not the ones with credit enough to be noticed. And who could I trust?"

"Then couldn't people come out your way—like you and I will?" It seemed so simple.

Jay said wearily, "The front door records every going in and coming out. I wouldn't like to guess how fast the alarms would go off in Admin when the third person stepped onto the street. And I don't want to find out."

"The real problem," said someone else, whom after a moment Gem recognized as Mike, "is fear. That's all. Ours, theirs. If they can push us down here once, they can do it again. And next time—"

There was a sharp rustle of movement. "Don't," Jay said. "It doesn't bear thinking of."

Somewhere in the distance a bell rang, six strokes, a pause, seven more. The thin sound faded quickly.

"Our turn for the window," Sophie said. She waved at someone: Sal, who came and pushed the chair. Mike, Theo, Robin. There was a face missing. "Where's J2?" Gem asked.

"Greenhouse work, the lucky beggar," someone said. "I could use a day in the sun."

Gem thought they must mean that J2 was outside. She followed the others, expecting any moment to feel fresh air on her face. Someone went to fetch Mel. They came out at the window where she had first met J2, where the lines of plants were.

As Strand Seven came down into the light, other people came toward them, passed, and went back into the tunnels. Gem was haunted by the idea that she had seen them before, as if these were ghosts or shadows from Upstream. The face of Morgan Smith from Admin leaped out of the dark toward her; Gem drew breath in a startled gasp, and then saw it was nobody she knew. Yet the thought that he, that anyone in Admin, might know she was down here haunted her. And there was still so much to find out.

Under *6* All the Houses

They all sat down by the window, except for Gem. Jay, with his back to the light, joined in the signed conversation between Sal and Sophie. Gem could see his hands moving, more clumsily than theirs, in that pattern of meaning that she could not understand. Yet she felt, watching them, as if she were eavesdropping, and turned away. The silence was lonely. Gem walked forward into the rows of plants. Presently she found J2, by a line of tomatoes.

"What are you doing?"

"Keeping an eye on our antiquated hydroponics," J2 said. "To make sure none of the aerators has stopped, or the water level plummeted, or anything else drastic. Also, squashing aphids." He suited his action to his words, and said in a tone of hollow melodrama, "When I die of boredom, they will write on my tombstone, 'He Was the Human Ladybird.' "

Gem giggled. It was a relief to be silly with someone. Jay was so witty, it was hard work to keep up with him. J2 smiled down at her. "Sew some black spots on that red sweater," he said, "and you can join me."

"It's a deal," said Gem, and J2 looked at her sadly.

"It isn't, of course," he said, "but it's a nice thought." Gem suddenly felt as if she were walking in a mist of loneliness. Without thinking, she put her hand out and touched J2's shoulder. He smiled again, moved away, and squashed some more aphids. "If we have to be here," he said, "let's make the best of what we have. I don't suppose you know the City was much bigger once, in the days when . . ."

"When what?" Gem asked.

"When people like me were still Upstream, for a start. When nobody worried—or not much—about the environment. There was such a time."

Gem said, "Isn't anything Admin says true?"

Another smile. "Who knows? I daresay it's never insisted the City was always the size it is now. Anyway, when Admin pulled in City Edge, after whatever it was that shrank the population and removed most of the natural resources, it left some things behind." J2 rounded the end of a line and began again in the other direction. "For some reason—probably financial—Admin never came back to clear the outlying houses, only cut off the services. Hydro tanks—there are more in Strand Six—and some solar panels. Eventually we wired them up again."

"So why don't you have more lights?"

J2 spoke patiently. If he thought Gem was a nuisance, he managed not to show it. "One, we don't have many bulbs; two, the panels are very old and they break down. We're always short of something. We can only just scrape together power for the aerators, and cooking, and warmth. Those are a higher priority than light."

"It is cold down here," Gem agreed. "It must be worse in winter."

"Not if we stay deep enough," J2 said. "You have to remember that underground temperature's constant." He sounded as if it were an ordinary thing, this living in the dark, under all the houses. Gem supposed that, for him, it was. She watched him, noticing the longish dark hair, the slightly lopsided way he stood. "I'm sorry I upset Mel," she said.

"There wasn't time to warn you," he said. "Never mind."

"I asked Jay what's wrong with her."

"Well, don't put it like that for a start." He smiled. "Another lesson in Downstream manners. As it happens, there is nothing wrong with Mel; not physically. She was born Upstream, and if she'd stayed there, all would most likely have been well."

"But what happened, then?"

"She was born," J2 said slowly, "with a strawberry birthmark across her face. It looked horrific, but it was going to vanish in a few years. Kate Avrassian tried to tell that to Mel's mother, but she obviously didn't believe her. Mel was found on the edge of the water a few days later. She was quite safe—she'd been packed in one of those safety floating cradles."

"You mean," Gem said incredulously, "her mother just—just sent her Downstream? How could she? How did she know?"

"How could she?" J2 shrugged. "I think she must have been off her head. How she knew—who can tell? Perhaps she only guessed." He sighed. "Mel was as happy as the rest of us, as far as that goes. Until the birthmark faded, and then someone told her how she came down here. After that, slowly, she shut herself in, or shut us out. We have to take care of her, but so what? We all look after each other."

Gem thought she might try another question. "J2," she said, "why don't you all just walk out? Where the river goes?"

"Some of us do. Downstream beyond." His voice sounded so strained and uncomfortable that Gem looked at him sharply.

"What did I say?" she asked.

"Never mind. I'd really rather not explain."

Gem opened her mouth, darted a look at J2, and closed it again. It seemed this answer wasn't going to come easy; and Jay had already warned her against talking about Downstream beyond.

Up and down the rows of plants they went, in silence.

After a long while that distant bell rang again: seven strokes, then eight. "End of garden duty," J2 said, sounding relieved. "Strand Seven back to its rooms." He swung around and strode toward the tunnel.

"Anyone would think you were pleased," Gem said.

J2 jumped a boulder in the path and helped her over it. "Which would you find worse?" he asked. "Comfort in the dark, not able to see what you were missing; or on the edge of light, with what you can't have staring you in the face?"

Gem put her hands in her pockets. "Which *is* worse?" she said.

J2 was silent for about twenty paces. Then he said, "Never the same two days running. Look, take my hand, it's dark around this bend."

"What do you do?" Gem asked. "In the dark?"

"Oh . . . sing. Tell stories. Teach ourselves. I help Sophie with her encyclopedias a lot of the time. She's compiling two. *Facts*—anything we might need to know. And *Opinions*."

"What opinions? And could you walk slower?" Gem said breathlessly. J2 said sorry and slowed down, but didn't answer the other question for a while. Then he said, "Things people have said about—people like us. Some in favor, some definitely not. A long time ago, mostly. It is nice to feel that once our existence was at least acknowledged." There was so much bitterness in his voice that Gem only just stopped herself from pulling her hand out of his. She had thought Jay was contradictory, but somehow he remained Jay underneath it all, whatever act he put on. She'd never met anyone whose moods could be so different—silly, sad, bitter—and all in an afternoon.

"What about other things?" she asked. "Things you need. Medicine. Whatever."

Jay would have pinned her down to a precise request; J2 said, as if he knew what she meant without asking, "Bill—Kate's partner, the one who works in the recycling plant—he scavenges for us: nuts, bolts, and other outmoded bits of technology. Kate passes them down."

"What about paper?"

"That too. And Jay brings some."

"But it's so hard to get hold of. And you let Mel play with it."

J2 stopped short, so that Gem cannoned into him. Then he let go of her hand. "Giving paper to Mel when she needs it is more important than what else we might want it for. Never mind how the world works Upstream. It's different here."

It was so dark. Gem reached out to where she thought J2's voice was coming from. Panic fluttered in her throat. "All right," she said, "I'm sorry. This is only my second time here."

J2 chuckled. "So it is. I should have learned patience enough by now." His hand touched her shoulder, down her arm, took her hand again.

They came into the wide space that was Strand Seven's group room. Away in the distance a line of light: Mel's lamp shining in her room of paper flowers. J2 said, "We'll go into what Sophie calls her office; then you can have a look at the encyclopedias." He led Gem through another brief honeycomb of passages, said, "Wait there a moment," and left her standing. Gem, straining her ears, heard him moving around. There was a click, and one of the glowworms lit, if light it could be called, this small circle of the darkness. Gem moved closer.

"*Facts,*" J2 said. *Facts* was a pile of large pages held together by a piece of string threaded through one corner, and at present open at a picture with instructions.

"What's a haybox?" Gem asked.

"How to cook without fuel, provided you can find a substitute for the hay and the box." J2 moved the glow-worm. *"Opinions."*

The *Opinions* encyclopedia was pinned, pasted, fastened somehow, all across the wall. The first thing Gem saw was the scrap of newsprint that had disappeared from the box the morning Jay had called up to her window from the street. She moved closer. Lines of verse, of prose; pages, scraps of paper; printed, handwritten.

There was nothing at all about Philippa to indicate her terrible affliction.

. . . who did sin, this man, or his parents, that he was born blind? Jesus answered, Neither hath this man sinned, nor his parents.

Society is no readier to accept crippledness than to accept death, war, sex, sweat, or wrinkles.

This language of the body
admits no irregular
constructions.
I have no interpreter.

. . . plan to use abortion and sterilization to prevent disabled babies has been condemned as "monstrous" . . .

What matters deafness of the ear, when the mind hears? The one true deafness, the incurable deafness, is deafness of the mind.

It's the cant of you folks to be horrified if a blind man robs, or lies, or steals; oh yes, it's far worse in him, who can barely live on the few halfpence that are thrown to him in the streets. . . . You who have five senses may be wicked at your pleasure; we who have four, and want the most important, are to love and be moral on our affliction. The true charity and justice of rich to poor, all the world over!

And thought the grave would cure me, and was glad
When the time came to lose what joy I had

And in that day shall the deaf hear the words of the book, and the eyes of the blind shall see out of obscurity, and out of darkness.

Then he wrote, "Regarding the child, rear it, if it is a boy; if it is a girl, expose it."

. . . they exclaim, "Of course they should be aborted! It is criminal to make a woman carry a deformed child."

My mind flies free as does my heart
Preserve me from those who shun me
Seeing only a thing in a chair or on sticks

The words flew like strange birds around the inside of Gem's mind. They spoke to her of things she had never known or imagined. She reached out for a book—a whole book, how old could it be?—that lay on the table. *"The Creatures Time Forgot,"* she read.

"That's us," J2 replied. She looked at him, real and smiling in the dim light. How did it feel to be forgotten? A little cold fist of horror clutched at her heart. If I come down here again, will I be forgotten too?

"Let's go somewhere else," she said.

"All right." J2 switched off the light and led her back into the group room. "Jay? Sophie?" he called.

"Down at the jetty," someone answered, and J2 set off again. Gem began to tire of the dark. She hankered after light and fresh air, to be able to talk without the pitfalls of wrong words and questions. She could only just tell that they were going in a different direction. The sound of their footsteps changed, and the feel of the ground under their feet. Now it wasn't stone, but sand. There was a faint noise of water, and the cold air moved.

"There they are," said J2, and Gem saw another light: Jay's flashlight, turned to its widest beam and stuck in the sand. The jetty was a black framework of wood, slimy with age and damp. It didn't look safe, but Jay was sitting on the edge of it swinging his legs, and Sophie was out on the end in her chair, looking upstream.

"It's us," J2 said, and sat down at the water's edge with his arm around his knees.

Gem picked her way carefully to where Sophie was sitting. "What's that way?" she asked.

"Nothing very much," Sophie said, without looking around. "A steep drop down from Upstream. The arch under City Bridge, if we could see it. I like to think it's there." She was combing the front bits of her hair with her fingers. "Looking to the Promised Land," she said, and began assiduously braiding her hair. "There is," she went on, "a legend, or a saying, or an idea, whichever you like, that when someone at last succeeds in climbing out of here by the upstream way, all our troubles will be over." She spun the wheelchair slowly on the awkward surface, stopped, and said, "Sit down, do. I strain my neck talking to you up there."

Gem sat on her heels and wondered if Sophie would ever get friendly enough to call her by her name. Cautiously she said, "What did you think of the map?"

"Useful," Sophie said. "Very useful." She pattered her fingers on the side of the wheelchair, and then said, "Jay, can you get a plan of the City sound lines? You know, the ones you message each other by? The music lines will do, failing that."

Jay looked around so sharply that Gem heard the joints in his neck click. "Whatever for?"

"Never mind," Sophie said, and then, "Well . . . why shouldn't you know, after all? We have it in mind to make a way out of here."

"You'll never do it," Jay said. Gem wondered why he was so certain of it. Almost as if he wanted to be certain. And then he said, "And anyway, why now?"

"Because I've grown old enough to want to," Sophie said. "Or because of the map. Or it's about time someone tried again, if there's been a before. Or the stars are right. *Anything.*" She smacked her hands together. "I've got to try at last, or go crazy."

Gem licked her lips nervously, and said, "I did wonder why you don't just go out where the river does."

There was a cold pause before Sophie replied. "Some do," she said. "We call it going Downstream beyond."

"What happens?"

"They don't come back. Maybe they drown. Who knows? We don't." She looked at Gem. "Did you ever hear of them? Do you know what is right away downstream beyond the City?"

"No," Gem said. "No. But somebody must know."

"Someone, somewhere, maybe," Jay said. "But it's the map that's worrying me."

"It looks accurate enough," Sophie said.

"No, it's not that." Jay slipped down off the edge of the jetty and landed with a splash in the shallow water. "I hunted and hunted for a map, years ago. How come Gem found it? How come it was there?"

"You might have overlooked it," Gem said. "The data banks are big enough."

"But you found it easily—*easily*," Jay said, his voice hard and anxious. "Supposing it was left there on purpose? As bait? So they know when someone's nosing around?"

"They think I shredded it," Gem reminded him.

"I hope they do." Jay splashed ashore. "I hope you know what you're doing, Sophie. Whatever you are doing. I wish you'd tell me."

"We can look after ourselves," Sophie said dryly.

"But trying to get out! With Admin maybe breathing down your necks? And ours?" Jay swung around toward her, his arms swinging wide. "It's madness!"

"Remember the agreement, Jay," his brother said.

Jay let his arms fall. He took two deep, rasping breaths, and said bitterly, "Oh, I *remember*!" J2 reached out his arm, but Jay turned away hurriedly and ran off. Gem didn't know whether she should go after him or not; it was an uncomfortable feeling, like being stranded in the middle of somebody else's family argument. Jay had left his flashlight behind; she stooped and picked it up. The light swung wildly, narrowed as she rubbed the controls, and settled on the edge of the water.

"You'd better take it back to him," Sophie said in a dull voice.

"I don't know the way back to his room. If he's gone that way at all."

J2 got up from the sand and said, "I'll take you back. Sophie?"

"Oh, send Sal down to push me up, please. Or someone else, if she's busy."

Gem followed J2 away and into the tunnels. "Will Sophie be all right?"

"Of course she will." J2 sounded as if he were swallowing down exasperation. "Look, Gem, you heard what I said to Jay about the agreement. It's the big rule here. Help isn't wanted until it's asked for. That applies to you and Jay and Kate and Bill more than to the rest of us, because we understand ourselves and you don't. However hard you try, you don't."

Gem didn't dare say any more. They walked silently, side by side, up the long dark tunnels, following the blob of light from the flashlight. The cold underground wind blew around them. At last they came to the foot of the slope that led to Jay's room. There was another glimmer in the distance: pale light through Jay's ceiling window, falling on the side of the tunnel.

"He shouldn't have left the door open," said Gem.

"You'll find your way now" was all J2 said.

"Why don't you—come and see Jay?" Gem blurted out.

"Don't tempt me," J2 said lightly. But he took one step up the slope. Then he said, "I have to send Sal down for Sophie," and walked away. Stopped again. "Gem," he said, not turning around.

"Yes?"

"Come back soon."

Slowly, swinging Jay's flashlight in her hand, Gem went up toward his room. Would he still be in a mood? He'd been so touchy with Sophie—almost as if he were afraid. *Could* he be afraid—and of what?

And what about yourself, if you had a brother down there? thought Gem, and another sudden cold thought made her stop short. Suppose . . . ? She shook her head. She couldn't ask anyone up here. But how ever, how *ever*, had Jay known he had a brother?

Jay was not in his room. Carefully Gem closed the door, fitted the panel back in the wall, laid the flashlight down on Jay's bed, and let herself out. It was a cool, dry day. And Jay had walked straight out of the house, not so long ago, without changing his shoes. Faint wet footprints on the paving.

"Strange, isn't it?"

"You!" said Gem, swallowing the gasp that had tried to leap out past her lips.

Morgan Smith grinned at her. "Don't look so frightened. Or were you expecting Jay?"

"I might have been."

"Funny, since you just came out of his house." He traced the outline of a damp patch with his foot. "What have the two of you been doing?"

"Fooling around, if you must know," Gem said, forcing herself to sound cool. "Jay got into the fountain."

"Oh yes; I'd forgotten their famous fountain. Anything else?"

"What business is it of yours?" Gem snapped, temporarily forgetting cool. "I don't suppose there's any law against walking in fountains."

"Shouldn't think they needed one," Morgan Smith said, and grinned again. "But never mind my business. Only, if you have had a lovers' tiff, I'd be interested."

"We have not," Gem said coldly, "had a lovers' tiff." There was no need to mention that she and Jay weren't in fact—but the amount of time she was spending at Jay's house it probably looked as if . . . To her fury Gem felt herself blushing scarlet. She glared at Morgan Smith. He was laughing at her.

"Don't slap me now," he said. "It'll cost you. I'm in uniform."

"Coward!" she retorted, and stalked off to look at the stream where it went in under City Bridge.

She leaned her elbows on the parapet and thought about the *Opinions* encyclopedia. It was an effort; those strange words escaped her in the light. They seemed real only in the other country: Downstream.

Gem wasn't seeing the water at all when Jay said, "Hi." She put her thoughts away in the back of her mind.

"You are a fool," she told him. "Huffing out of the house—not that that matters—but leaving wet footprints on a dry day for all the world to see."

"All the world being?"

"Me, and Morgan Smith from Admin, for a start." Gem scuffed her toes against the bridge. "Anyone would think you wanted someone to find out about—" She glanced around. Nobody in earshot. "Downstream."

"No! Of course not." Jay leaned back against the bridge. "How did you choke Morgan Smith off?"

"Larking around in your fountain." Gem looked sideways up at Jay; he was frowning, but in a thoughtful way, not angrily. Prompted by she didn't know what, Gem went on, "He asked if we'd had a lovers' tiff."

She expected Jay to laugh. He didn't, but the frown smoothed away from his forehead. He swung around and propped his elbows on the parapet, next to hers. "You mean he thinks we—"

"I guess he must," Gem said casually, wishing she'd kept her mouth shut.

"Shame for a good honest Admin man to be mistaken." Jay moved a little closer to her. "What about it?"

Gem shifted over. "Leave it, Jay." She took care not to look at him.

There was a longish pause before Jay said, "Why?" His arm went around her shoulders. She smacked it off.

"Don't."

"Why not, Gem?" Jay asked, and then she remembered his own words to her, so few days ago.

"Would 'Because I asked you' be a good-enough reason?" she demanded.

Jay raised his eyebrows. "All right," he said. "Call it quits. But I do wish there were a reason I could get hold of."

"So do I," Gem said. There wasn't, not that she could think of. If it was only Jay she had to deal with, it would have been easy—to say yes, for example. But what with

Downstream, and Admin, and all the unspoken secrets, life was suddenly very complicated. "I'm sorry," she said.

"You don't have to apologize."

"I just can't think straight anymore."

"Poor Gem," Jay said.

Gem sighed. She wanted life to be back to normal. But Downstream was like a drug: new, strange, exciting. "Jay!" she said in a quick whisper, because someone was walking along the Edge toward them. "We'll go—you know where—again?"

"Whenever you like," Jay said. He drew even closer to her as the walker came by. Chris Peters from Admin, patrolling City Edge. He smiled, nodded, walked on by.

"I don't like him," Gem said.

"Don't think about him, then," Jay said. "Think about Downstream."

Like a drug: dangerous.

7
Cement

Not as often as Gem liked, but often enough, she and Jay went Downstream. Some nights Jay's parents were away, in Central Admin if his father had business, or at City Two if his mother was singing in a concert. Then Gem walked to Jay's house in the evening. They went Downstream and stayed the night, sleeping on the sandy floor with J2 and the others from Strand Seven. Gem would come out again and be surprised to find the City daylit, or walk nervously through the City streets feeling as if the air of Downstream must be around her like some cold perfume.

Meanwhile, Downstream, whatever plan Sophie had was on the move. Suppressed tension burst out among the Waterbound in flares of temper or hysterical laughter. And neither J2 nor Sophie would tell what the plan was, even after Jay brought Sophie the map of the City sound lines that she had asked for. Only Mel seemed untouched by the restless atmosphere, and sat in her room folding paper flowers. She never said anything, but smiled when Gem sat down beside her, and took Gem's hands to show her how to make the intricate fine folds.

"It's so strange," Gem said to Jay once. "Keeping this huge secret."

"Not so strange to me," Jay said. "I've kept it twelve years."

At last Gem visited the Waterbound on her own. It was odd to walk in through the door of Jay's house as if she lived there, and find her own way to his room and the tunnel, all in deserted silence. Jay's flashlight was clipped in its usual place against the skylight, with its power unit toward the sun. Although the tunnels were beginning to seem familiar, she didn't yet dare to walk alone in the dark.

She met Mike first, doing scout duty on the outer fringes. He turned his face toward the sound of her footsteps. "Who's that?"

"Gem Rannesen." She knew he couldn't see her, but she didn't like not to smile. "I thought I might go and talk to J2."

"He's probably along at the jetty with Sophie," Mike said. "Can you find your way?"

Gem wasn't sure, but she said, "Yes, thanks," all the same. She found the way to the group room, and followed the tracks of a wheelchair from there. Only Robin and Sophie in Strand Seven used chairs, so there was a fifty percent chance she had taken the right path.

Her luck was in. The chair was Sophie's, and J2 was with her. They were both in the river, swimming.

"Aren't you freezing?" Gem demanded.

"What, working this hard?" J2 kicked himself ashore, scrambled up, and shook the long dark hair from his eyes. In Gem's flashlight the drops swung away from him like bright beads of glass. It was the first time Gem had seen him with bare shoulders; she tried not to look. The left shoulder, which had no arm, was disturbing, like a broken statue. Shut up, she said to herself inside her head. It's J2. You've talked to him often enough. Sophie's arms gleamed like leaping fish as she swam across and grabbed hold of the jetty.

"Give me a heave up, 2."

J2 reached down, and in a moment Sophie was sitting on the edge of the jetty, her legs dangling in the water.

Gem sat beside her. "Is it deep?"

"Deep enough." Sophie shook her hair back as J2 had,

and it flicked across Gem's face in wet black snakes.

"Two mermaids side by side," murmured J2.

"Yes," Sophie agreed. "But only one of us with flippers."

There was a dry chuckle from J2. Gem said, "I read a story about a mermaid. She gave her voice for a pair of legs."

"Yes," Sophie said, "and it felt as if she were walking on knives. Me, I'd keep my voice."

"I wonder what Sal would do," J2 said, and added, "Where's Jay, Gem?"

"Gone to City Two for a concert."

"Is Ma singing?"

"I don't know." Gem looked away. "I should think so."

"I remember her singing. It was great. I still miss it." J2 sat for a moment and then said, "I do go up Jay's tunnel sometimes. Squash my ears against the door in case I can hear her singing. I did once."

"You remember?" Gem said. "But I thought—" She wasn't quite sure what she thought. Only she had assumed that J2, like all the others, knew of no life except Downstream. "J2," she said, "were you ever—"

"That'll do," Sophie said sharply. Gem glanced at J2. He had turned his back to her.

There was a plop in the dark waters of the river. A good excuse to change the subject. "What was that?"

"Fish," Sophie said.

"Supper," J2 added. "If it swims into the right net." He picked up a piece of what looked like sacking and began to towel himself vigorously. "Do my arm for me, Soph?"

"If you'll do my feet." Sophie looked around. "Gem, since you're here, you can help me into the chair." So she had called Gem by name at last; but nobody could call it being friendly. And besides—

"Me? I mean, how?" Gem stammered.

"You are strong enough to pick me up?" Sophie asked, at her most sardonic.

"Well, I expect so, but I don't get asked to do this sort of thing every day."

"Keep your hair on," Sophie muttered, and then, surprisingly, grinned. "Just do it how you like, so long as it works."

"Is that all right?" Gem asked, panting, a few minutes later.

"Not bad for a first time." Sophie took the towel from J2 and dried his arm. Then he knelt down and dried her feet. Gem stood by, feeling useless and a little embarrassed.

J2 flashed a brief glance at her and said, "What's the matter?"

"Nothing."

Sophie said under her breath, "Doesn't like seeing us flashing our differences around."

J2 chuckled and said, "So she should be thankful I'm wearing shorts." They laughed together, and Gem felt excluded, left out. But that's what I am, she thought: an outsider, an Upstreamer. I just have to hope they'll invite me in, one day.

"However," Sophie said, "this wet shirt isn't doing much for my modesty. Come on, 2, dry clothes."

The bell rang for time at the window as they went down the tunnel toward Strand Seven, in the luxury of light from the flashlight Gem was carrying. J2 asked, "What's the day like, outside?"

"Bright. Sunny," Gem replied.

J2 walked on for a few paces in silence, then said, "Sophie, let's go along to the window and dry off there. Or we'll miss our time."

Without a word Sophie turned her chair aside, into the stream of people from Strand Six coming back from the window. Gem saw again the face she thought she had recognized before. "Who's that?" she said. "Over there, standing at the side."

"Owen," Sophie said. "Why?"

"He looks like Morgan Smith from Admin." They were going past him by now. Gem glanced sideways. As she looked, Owen pushed himself upright and walked away with a rigid, stiff-legged gait. "Owen Smith,"

Sophie said. "Used to be with us till last year when he and Fliss Corby paired. He's in Strand Six now."

They went on down to the window. Gem wanted to ask questions but was half frightened what the answers might be. At last she said, "What's your other name, Sophie?"

"I don't know," Sophie said. "I never wanted to know. Would you?"

"Yes," Gem said.

"Why?" Sophie asked. "So you had someone to blame?" There was something like a sneer in her voice.

"I'd want to know who I was."

"I know that well enough without a family name," Sophie said.

"What about Sal?"

"Sal Brenault."

Gem stopped short, and J2 bumped into her. With a muttered apology Gem went on again, but if she followed Sophie, it was more by luck than judgment, for she wasn't watching where she was going. She was running her memory back. How long had she known Jay? How long had she known Ness Brenault? The answer came: Jay introduced Ness to you a month after you first met him. Jay and J2; Ness and Sal; Gem and—no. Surely not. Surely.

They rounded the last corner and came into the light that shone through the deep window. There were a hundred questions humming in Gem's ears, but the only one she asked was, "Who do you ask? If you want to know who you are?"

"Kate," Sophie said, and waved. There was Sal, sitting beside Robin in the dusty sunshine at the foot of the window, the light glinting on her red hair. Now that she knew, Gem thought, She does look like Ness. Just a little bit.

Sophie said suddenly, "As it happens, Kate doesn't know who my parents are anyway, so that solves the problem for me. I'm one of the Moses babies."

"What?" Gem sat down next to Sal.

Sophie cast her eyes up. "I thought you had faith lines in your houses Upstream," she said. "I came Downstream in the modern equivalent of a basket of reeds, without recourse to Kate. Just like Melanie."

"Yes, J2 told me that."

Sophie said, in a measured voice that revealed precisely nothing, "The difference being, of course, that whoever my mother was, she kept well out of the system."

Carefully, Gem said, "Sophie—can I ask—"

"You can always ask. I may not answer."

"Do you think your mother, or Mel's, knew about the Waterbound?"

"I really—" Sophie said, swallowed, and tried again. "I really don't know. Perhaps there is some kind of legend, a secret line of rumors. But what, where, who, I couldn't tell you." She turned on Gem with a flashing smile. "Did your ma never try to frighten you with the bogeys?"

"Not Ma." Gem swallowed. "Pa did. He used to say they'd come through the floor and grab me." How many people knew, or guessed, and how much? Or did they think it was an urban myth, like the ancient ancient one of alligators in the sewers, some other place, some other time? Gem stared at Sal, who had perched herself on the arm of Robin's chair and was signing fast. She looked around for J2. He was curled up on the floor, asleep.

Sophie actually smiled. "He's tired. We've been exploring new tunnels since we got your map. There aren't enough of us to live in all of them, but it's nice to know they're there."

"Can—" Gem hesitated. I don't want her to think I'm trying to take over. "Could I come too, sometime?"

"Don't see why not. Yes, come again tomorrow." Sophie smiled again. "Good-bye, Gem."

Gem got to her feet and walked back to Jay's room. Up into the light again, back to real life. Home to her own house, and Pa saying, "Oh, you *are* still alive. I was beginning to wonder." He ignored her when she was there; couldn't he ignore her when she wasn't? A sizzling message on line from Ness: "What about the project, Rannesen—it's supposed to be both of us working, isn't it?"

With an effort Gem opened line to college and listened to the songs Ness had recorded for the project. Ness must be interested to work on it at all; and Gem hadn't known she could sing like that. There are all sorts of things I don't know about Ness. Such as Sal. She tidied up the text, added some more conclusions, and sent it down line again with "Satisfied?" tagged on. It seemed ages since she had been in her room, or on line. It felt strange. Gem moved over to the window. There was Morgan Smith in the street below. With an irritated thump she darkened the glass and went to bed, waiting for tomorrow as if she were a child with a birthday and Downstream for a present. Waiting, she realized, to see J2 again. And Jay, of course, don't forget Jay. . . .

Morgan Smith was outside again next morning, and it was evening before Gem could escape to Jay's tunnel. An hour later she and J2 and Sal were somewhere none of them had been before.

J2 said vaguely, "I think we're too far over. Let's stop and have a look."

Gem's map of the City and the water was more crumpled than ever, and smudgy with fine sand. There was a charred place at one edge where someone had held it too close to a candle, and the creases where it folded were nearly worn through. Gem saw that Jay's map of the sound lines had been carefully traced onto it. There were lines to mark the passages explored; most of them snaked around the node points in the sound line system.

They put their heads together over the map while Sal held the candle. Candles were rare; this one, and the two spares, were a piece of special pleading. Jay's flashlight, which Gem had brought down as usual, was on loan to Robin in the workshop.

"We're there, aren't we?" Gem said, pointing.

"There, I think," J2 said. Sal only shrugged, making the candle flame dip and flicker.

"Oh help," J2 said. "I'm going to sit down and brood over it. I could use a rest."

Sal stuck the candle in the ground, and Gem sat down too, wriggling until she had her back against the side of the tunnel. J2 was sitting with his eyes shut, tracing lines on the sand with one finger.

Gem couldn't get comfortable; something was sticking into her back. She twisted around and tried to scrape it smooth with her hands.

"J2," she said.

"What?"

"This is hard. It's rock."

J2 crawled toward her, stopping once to beckon Sal forward. He waited until she had brought the candle nearer, put his hand on the rock, and then took the candle from Sal and held it close to the gray, pitted surface.

"It's not rock," he said. "Cement."

"I thought they didn't use that anymore," Gem said.

"Maybe." The candlelight flickered again and again. J2's hand was shaking. He turned his head and looked at Sal; a shift of her head meant she was signing, her hands hidden behind J2. He nodded: once, twice.

"Hold that," he said, and gave Gem the candle. He and Sal began to rub and rub at the sandy earth, freeing it from the cement. J2 knelt lopsided to keep his balance, pushing at the gritty stuff with his hand.

"Shall I help?" Gem asked.

"No," J2 said fiercely. "You leave it alone." So Gem sat back on her heels and watched. The cement was pocked with pits and holes. With a shock of recognition Gem saw a handprint, smacked deep into it. She came nearer. Two holes close together were the marks of fists, slammed down. A bigger hole with a hump of cement below, as if someone had tried to claw it out before it set. Several sets of hands, different sizes, as if a group of people had been digging frantically to get something out.

Sal grunted as a shower of dust slithered into her hair. She stood up and began to move her arms in wide sweeping arcs against the wall. More dust fell, and a flat surface was revealed. On it someone had written two names. The cement must have been almost set then, for the letters were shallow. After the names was a date. "Sixty years ago," whispered J2.

He and Sal huddled together, signing in the light of the candle. Gem felt shut out by their closeness. She didn't like to think what that pockmarked cement face might mean.

"Come on," said J2. "We're going back." He took Gem's arm and pulled her away. Gem, looking back over her shoulder, saw Sal light one of the precious spare candles and push it into the sandy floor. She didn't look at Gem when she came back; but Gem saw tears on her face.

J2 was in a hurry: Sometimes they were moving so fast that the flame of the candle Sal was carrying nearly went out. At last he slowed, and the grim set of his face relaxed. "I've got to think," he said. "I must tell Sophie." He tapped Sal's arm: a flicker of signs. Then Sal leaned against the wall, cupping her hand around the candle flame and watching the shining light.

"J2," Gem said, "what was—that? What were they trying to dig out?"

"Not what," J2 said, "but who." Gem's heart gave a

sick lurch inside her. "It's a tomb," J2 went on. "We've all heard stories—I never knew for sure it really happened till now." He looked at Gem. "I don't particularly want to tell you. It's our story."

"I'd like to know." Gem said, trying not to let her voice wobble.

J2 bit his bottom lip. "Oh well," he said. "You saw the date. It was then. They say Ken was—oh, thirty, I suppose. He was deaf. Gina was a few years younger; she was expecting their baby. They were desperate to have the baby Upstream—they thought they could make sure somehow that the baby at least had a life there." J2 hesitated, and went on. "Ken was digging through in a deserted place. They did tell a few friends; not enough, or they might have been stopped from going. And we can only guess, someone must have found out Ken was digging. He broke through to Outside and went back down to help Gina. And then, when they were crawling through—" J2 stopped again. "You saw the cement. So did their friends, but it was too late."

Gem couldn't say anything. She was too caught up in the story. J2 had told it as if it had happened to people he knew, though he had not been born then: and to think of that happening to friends—the sudden, cold, wet, suffocation . . . "Do you think they knew?" she stammered.

"I shouldn't think it knocked them out before it

choked them, no," J2 said savagely. "Do you wonder we're in two minds about trying to get out?"

"It's horrible!" Gem cried. "It shouldn't happen—you shouldn't be down here at all!"

"Hey, ssh," J2 said. "Much more of this and I shall begin to think you care."

"Why shouldn't I care?" said Gem. She felt helpless, desperate to do something that might help; and all she could think of was to put her arms around J2. She felt him twitch with surprise; then he put his hand on her shoulder and pushed her away. "Candlelight's all very well," he said, "but this is hardly the time."

Gem stepped back, stammering, "I didn't mean— I'm sorry."

J2 smiled. "Of course you didn't," he said. "Neither did I. My bad idea of a joke. Shall I take you back?"

"Yes, please."

Sal blew out the candle, and the darkness came down again. Gem felt her hand taken. There was grit on J2's palm, a memory of that cement wall between them as they walked.

J2 stopped at the usual place and said, "There you are."

Gem said, "Come to the door with me."

"Your voice is all shaky," J2 said.

"*I'm* all shaky. That was horrible." Gem felt J2 pat her shoulder. He said, "All right. I'll come with you."

He was still behind her when she knelt down to open the door and undo the panel, and when she crawled through into Jay's room, but he didn't come any farther. He did bend down, to get a look through Jay's skylight. It was dark by now, and the stars were shining. Gem, still on her knees, turned back.

J2 put his hand out, slowly, as if the air in the room might be dangerous. Then he bit his lip and drew back. "Gem," he said, "here's another of my hopeless jokes. Come again soon."

"I don't know." At the moment Gem felt as if she wanted to blot the whole of Downstream from her memory.

"It's not all horror stories," J2 said, and froze as the key plate on Jay's door buzzed.

It was Jay himself, back from City Two. He smiled at Gem, slung his bag on the bed, and whistled when he saw J2 inside the tunnel. But he said nothing.

"You don't mind?" J2 said.

"Why should I?" Jay grinned. "Go all the way, come right through."

"Come on, 2," Gem urged, but it was Jay who said suddenly, "On second thought, better not. The house would register someone who didn't come through the door."

An idea began to bubble in Gem's brain. "Do you

mean," she said, "as a different person, or as an extra body?"

"Oh, the extra body," Jay said lightly. "I don't think we're that top level as to be specific."

"Then," Gem said, the idea now fizzing merrily, "why don't you change places for a day?" She was aware of them both staring at her, then at each other.

"And supposing my parents came in?" Jay asked, his voice sounding dry and slightly breathless.

"Pick some time when they're not here. Lock the door. Don't you know how alike the two of you sound?"

"True enough." Jay turned his face toward the dark mouth of the tunnel. "What say, 2?"

"Words fail me." A long pause. "Yes, if Gem will keep me a bit of company." J2 let his breath out abruptly. "Come on, Jay, shut the wall. Let me know when." As Jay picked up the painted panel, Gem heard his brother say, "Was it a good concert? Was Ma singing?"

"Yes. Top level."

There was a long pause. J2 said, "Good-bye, then," and they heard him walking away. Slowly Jay pushed the panel to. It closed with a sharp click. He stared at it for a moment and then frantically clawed it down again, pushed the door open, and shouted for J2 to come back. There was no reply. Jay sat up and wiped the back of his hand across his mouth.

"He must have heard me." Once more he closed off the tunnel. "He must have heard me," he said again, and sat on his heels, staring blindly in front of him.

"What did you want?" Gem asked.

"I wanted him to come back," Jay said. "I wanted to say good-bye properly. I never do. I ought to." Then he hissed, as if something hurt, and looked around frantically.

"Jay, what's wrong?"

"I forgot Admin might be listening." Jay banged his forehead against the wall. "I'm getting careless, *careless*."

As if on cue, the red light flickered by the screen. Jay stared at it, then made a face. He stood up. "Where's my flashlight?"

"I lent it to—" Gem said, and stopped her tongue just in time. Cover up with a sneeze. "I lent it out," she said, "and forgot it."

"Oh well," Jay said. "No matter. They say it's going to be bright tomorrow. How about going Outside?"

Gem would have liked to go Outside. But she wasn't sure if she could take another afternoon with Jay, if he was going to be so intense. So she said, "Not this time, thanks," and went home, trying to persuade herself she wouldn't have enjoyed it anyway. But once I wouldn't have minded. When life was simple, before I knew J2. She found herself thinking about J2, not Downstream, but

Upstream. Running across the grass the way she had with Jay. Holding her hand.

Don't be stupid. You can't have it, so shut up wanting. It only hurts.

Marking Time

A week passed. Gem didn't go near Jay's house, nor seek him out. She pushed her work quota up again, and conferred politely with Ness on the best presentation for "Protest Songs of the Nineteenth to the Twenty-First Centuries"; and she was horribly bored.

When at last she palmed herself into Jay's room, he looked around incuriously from his work, painting the panel again. "Oh, it's you. I was beginning to wonder."

Gem bounced on the bed. "You sound like my pa."

"I take it that's not a compliment." Jay smiled. "Never mind." He dabbed at the panel with the brush.

Gem looked for the flickering red light. Not a sign of it. "Did you get your flashlight back?"

"No, I bought another one. Seemed easiest." Jay stared at the painting as if willing it into submission and took up a smaller brush. "That lamp Mel has in her room was mine once." He leaned forward.

"What are you painting?"

"See for yourself." It was a tree. Gem thought it was beautiful, light and green and shade brought together. But Jay, after an intense silence, said, "Dead wood," and moved away. He put the brushes to clean and said, "It's J2's birthday tomorrow."

Gem said, "Happy birthday, J2."

"Will you come down?" Jay asked, sounding diffident, nervous: not sounding like Jay.

"If you want me to."

He looked at her and nodded, then said, "J2 asked."

"Oh." An unexpected warm glow in Gem's inside. She shrugged it off and said, "It's nice to be appreciated."

"And—Gem, could you make a cake? I know you can."

Gem, taken aback, said, "I'll try." She looked at the time, glowing on Jay's wall. "If it's for tomorrow, I'd better go and see if I've got credit for two eggs and four each butter, flour, sugar."

Jay laughed, as if she'd unknotted some bundle of tension inside him. "Bless you, Gem. Tomorrow."

Cakes were the only thing Gem could cook. Everything else came needing heating only, except for the vegetables from the vegetable patch, and those were too precious—Ma wouldn't let her touch them. In the end, because she had the credit and because Ma would like it—perhaps Pa would too, but he wouldn't say so—Gem made two cakes, one for her parents and one for Jay's brother.

She slipped out of doors early next morning. The fine weather was on the edge of breaking; leaves chased her ankles around street corners in the wind, and her hair whipped across her face.

Jay must have woken even earlier; he had already gone Downstream. Gem found them, with a little help from Mike and Theo, in J2's cubbyhole. Jay's flashlight was shining faintly; Jay himself was lounging on a heap of ragged blankets. J2 was sitting in the way that was now familiar, his arm wrapped across his chest and holding his shoulder.

"There you are," Jay said. J2 just turned his head and smiled.

"Happy birthday," Gem said awkwardly, and held out the cake.

"Hey," J2 said. "Thanks. This is great. All it needs is candles." Jay chuckled and held out a loosely wrapped packet. "Happy birthday. I'm afraid they're too big to stick in the cake."

J2 unwrapped the packet and out fell four honey-colored, honey-scented candles. He picked one up and sniffed it. "Mmm. Who did you sell your soul to?"

"Head of Admin's wife. She keeps bees. Respectable antiquarian pursuit." Jay grinned.

They were so alike, Gem thought, when they were together. Apart, she knew the difference. And what about J2's arm? a voice in her head asked, and the answer came back before Gem could think about it: That doesn't count. She blinked.

Jay was lighting one of the candles with the flashlight, which was the latest Upstream gadget, flashlight and heater and lighter in one. The two dark heads leaned closer as J2 held the candle and Jay the light; the flame flared, shrank, steadied, and shone clear. Everyone smiled.

Jay switched off the flashlight. J2 said, "Did anybody think to bring a knife?"

Gem had remembered. They cut the cake and munched in the honey-scented candlelight.

"Mm . . . m," J2 said. "Heaven."

"Near enough," Jay agreed, after a moment, in a voice that seemed to Gem both wry and bitter. Maybe J2 heard it as well; at any rate he said, "What's the trouble, Jay?"

Jay's reply came swift and vehement. "Only if this is heaven for you, what have I done to be living Upstream when by rights you should be with me?"

"Let that pass," J2 said.

"How?" Jay said. "How? Tell me that!" He stumbled to his feet. *"Oh—"* he said.

"Look here," J2 said. "I don't want my birthday spoiled. You sit down. Finish your cake and shut up complaining."

Jay stayed where he was, his fists clenched and his body taut with anger. J2 twisted around from his place on the floor to face him. He said something, softly, that Gem couldn't hear.

Jay glanced at Gem and suddenly relaxed. "Your wish is my command, O brother." He sat down with a sigh and leaned back against the wall. "This is a good cake."

J2 was carefully picking crumbs from his clothes and eating them. "Isn't it just? You must have sold your soul to Gem as well."

"No," Jay said. "Head of Admin's wife got all of it. Gem can have my body."

J2 looked at Gem. "If she wants it," he said.

Jay smiled lazily at Gem. "Well?"

"Who do you think I am?" Gem said. "Ness Brenault or someone? No." But at the same time she had a sudden vision of herself and Jay—no. Or maybe? J2 was still looking at her. Perhaps— *"No,"* Gem said again, less sure of herself than ever.

Jay shrugged and settled down more comfortably, but

presently he said, "I brought Mel some more paper. Better take it to her before I forget."

When they were alone, J2 watched the candle flame for a while, then said, "Has Jay changed his mind about swapping places for a day?"

"Not that I know of," Gem said, "but he doesn't always bother to say, when he changes his mind."

J2 nodded. "He hasn't said anything, and then you didn't come for a week. I almost wish you hadn't had the idea—now I feel as if I'm just marking time down here till Jay and I can swap, and that'll only be one day; and what then?"

"Don't worry about then," Gem said. "Enjoy now."

He smiled. "Very philosophical!" They talked until Jay came back, and Gem followed him as usual up the tunnel to his room. To her surprise Jay stopped before they were anywhere near the door, and said abruptly, "Gem, I've got two overnight passes for Outside off Pa. Will you come?"

"Oh yes!" was Gem's immediate reaction, and then, "Why?"

"To celebrate J2's birthday," Jay said. "I don't celebrate my own. Late autumn—who wants a birthday then? Boring time of year. You will come?"

"Yes," Gem said.

And so, next day, they went to the monorail terminal. One line to City Two, one line to nowhere. Jay loaded the pack, once the supervisor had checked it for anything that might damage the environment, and climbed in after Gem. A few minutes later the supervisor tapped on the glass and, when Jay lowered it, said, "Now remember. When you get to the end, a card will eject there." He pointed to the dashboard. "Don't lose it. It's set to direct you back to that terminal. It'll bleep if you go too far away to get back in time, and continuously for five minutes when it's time for you to start back. If you get to the terminal early, there's a slot you can put the card in to call the mono. Understood?"

"Perfectly," Jay said. The supervisor moved away. With an unexpected, silent whoosh the mono shot off, and Gem rocked in her seat.

"Want the glass up?" Jay shouted against the rush of air.

"No!" she shouted back. This was wonderful, like riding the wind. Gem shut her eyes and imagined she could fly. She had never traveled so fast in her life.

At the other end they climbed out. The monorail stretched like a silver wire back into the distance. The City was out of sight. They were on a low hill, the highest place they could see for miles around. The grass shimmered in the breeze. There were a few clumps of bushes.

"Come on," Jay said.

"Where?" Gem turned in a slow circle, looking. One grassy rolling landscape was much like another.

"Pick a direction."

Gem stuck her hand out at random. Jay gave her the batteries for the microstove to sling across her back where the sun would shine on them, and they set off.

Hours later Gem said, "I've never walked so far, ever."

"Have I tired you out? You should have said."

"Yes, but it's wonderful. It's worth it." Gem unslung the battery strap and flopped down in the grass. The sky above was deep, deep blue, tinged with purple toward the west, where the sun was setting. "It's so beautiful," Gem said. "It hurts."

"Mmm." Jay sat down on the pack that held the overnight tent and the microstove. Neither of them said anything else for a long time, until it was almost dark, and then Jay said, "Hungry?"

"Not much," Gem said, surprised.

"Me neither." Jay pulled things out of the pack. "Still, let's have something." He set up the stove and slotted in one of the batteries. A warm glow shone on them, light as well as heat. "Pot luck," Jay said, shoved a couple of canisters into the stove and fingered a control.

While they were waiting, he said, "And how do you like Downstream now you know it better?"

"There are still things I don't know," Gem answered.

"Of course." Jay sat up, hugging his knees. "First time I came Outside overnight, I was trying to get away from Downstream. It didn't work."

"What do you mean?"

"I can forget the City if I try hard enough," Jay said. "I can't forget Downstream."

Gem thought about that for a moment. It was true. The City was just a blur; she would have been happy to stay Outside forever, if she could. But the thought of Downstream was like a thread to pull her back. She said, "Did J2 tell you about what we found? About Ken and Gina?"

"Yes," Jay said.

"It was horrible."

"Yes," he said again. "Doesn't bear thinking about."

"I get so worried," Gem burst out, "in case Admin tries to do that again. In case Admin knows all about them."

"Shall I tell you a secret?" Jay said.

Gem looked at him quickly. "Jay—they *don't* know, do

they?"

He shook his head. "That's not the secret. This is. All Admin's efforts are directed strictly toward preserving the status quo. Keeping things how they are. They don't want to be forced to act. Because I don't think"—he spoke more slowly, weighing his words— "I don't think, though I'm not altogether sure, that they can afford to do anything else." He put his hand briefly on Gem's arm. "As for what you're afraid of: If anyone, even if only one, from Admin really knows what's Downstream, then he—or she—won't want the whole City knowing about it. And doing something about the tunnels is hardly going to go unnoticed."

"I suppose that's right," Gem said. "But Jay, there's so much I don't know."

Jay said, almost gently, not in his usual dry tone, "So what else don't you know, Gem?"

"Please tell me," Gem said, "how come you found out J2 was your brother, and about the tunnel."

"I always knew J2 was my brother," Jay said. "He wasn't always Downstream. He lived in the City for six years."

Gem bent a little closer over the warmth of the stove. "And nobody knew?"

"No," Jay said. "Ma could afford to pay not to have the tests, to have a home delivery. Which is to say, Bethan knew, Kate's predecessor. And—did he ever tell you he was one of twins?"

Gem shook her head.

"The younger one died. Bethan went back to the hospital and registered a single stillbirth. Ma fitted up the basement for a nursery. It wasn't wired into the rest of the house then. She did her best. She couldn't let him outside. I think she hoped that, Pa being who he was, 2 would be . . . allowed to stay." Jay was speaking in a quiet, even voice; only the sudden pauses, searching for the precise degree of unconcern, betrayed him.

"What happened?" Gem asked, half fearful of sparking off some wild outburst but wanting, more than anything, to know the answers now.

"She found out," Jay said, "that Pa being who he was, she had even less chance of keeping J2 than she thought." There was a long pause. "Go on," Jay said, "ask," and the old dry bitterness was back in his voice.

"How did they find out?" Gem whispered.

"It was my fault," Jay said. "It was my fault." Gem leaned forward to reach for Jay's hand, and found her own hand taken in a hard grasp. Jay drew in his breath. "I was born a year after J2. I always wanted him to be with me, do what I did. His arm—" Jay's voice faltered. "I thought maybe lots of people were like that." His grip tightened on Gem's hand. "I was five. It was a hot day; I wanted J2 to come into the garden." Gem's fingers were almost numb, but she kept quiet. "He was always so willing to please. Heaven help us, we never thought. Someone saw us from one of the high-rises and reported Ma that afternoon." Jay was breathing hard, as if he had been running. He fell silent.

"Jay," Gem said. "Jay, you're hurting my hand."

"Sorry." He let go. "I didn't realize what I'd done. There weren't hundreds of callers. Only someone came next day and took J2, to the hospital Ma said, he was ill. And the next day . . ." Jay hugged his knees to his chest. "They really did say he was ill. And then they told Ma they hadn't been able to save him. Whether she believed them . . . she never said anything else. She couldn't make me see J2 wasn't coming back. So I took off on my own to the hospital."

The stove pinged, making Gem jump. Jay leaned over and peeled the tops from the two canisters. "The label says mushroom soup."

"Mine has a mushroom in it," Gem said, looking.

"We can believe it? Wow." Jay blew on his soup and took a cautious mouthful. "By some . . . quite undeserved, amazing coincidence," he went on, "I wound up in Bethan's section before anyone stopped me. Only it was Kate's by then—she'd been in the job six months. She talked to me for a long, long time. And then she took me down to see J2."

"Down her tunnel?" Gem wiped her fingers around the soup can and licked them clean.

"It wasn't hers. Or even Bethan's. It's ancient—it's always been in the office, and the office goes with the job. Kate says it's an old incinerator chute." Jay's face twisted. "For—remains." He upended his canister and emptied it into his mouth. "Kate went to a lot of trouble for me," he said. "She fixed me up with therapy, given—given the circumstances. Only instead of talking to her, I went Downstream and talked to J2. Talked and talked, because Upstream I was too scared to say a word about it. When I was thirteen, I moved into J2's old room, put a homing device on the wall, and started tunneling up from below, from the Waterbound territory. It took months. I was that determined."

"Didn't your parents suspect?" Gem wondered if Jay would reply, but in the end he said, "I think they love me dearly. They give me anything I ask for. They turn a blind eye to anything I do. Though I do wonder sometimes whether they notice anything."

"Oh, surely . . ." Gem said, and Jay laughed.

"You know Ma. Wandering around in a fog of song. And Pa hardly home at all. Maybe they try to make up to me for . . . for being the only one. Or they try to forget." Jay ripped the tops off two more packets with unnecessary force. "One way or another I do not care. Fruit-flavored cream—help yourself."

The fruit had a sharp aftertaste: synthetic, not the real

thing. Jay said, "Well, that was a mistake." Another deep breath. "The story of my life."

"And I never knew," Gem said, wondering.

"No, well, how would you?" Jay said. "But I'm glad you know. I've been beginning to want somebody else. Kate wasn't enough to talk to. Sometimes I thought I'd explode. So thanks."

"For what?"

"Listening." Jay took hold of her hand, and said, "Gem, can I—?"

"Can you what?" Gem said, shivering a little, sure enough of what he meant. Jay leaned forward, put his other hand to her face, and kissed her. Then he rested his face in the angle of her neck and shoulder.

"Your neck smells of roses," he said, muffled.

"Jay," Gem said, "don't."

"Whyever not?"

"It's the first time—"

"I refuse to believe this is the first time you've been kissed," Jay said.

"No, but—this isn't what I came out here for."

"Plans can change."

"Jay!" Gem said. "Don't spoil it. Don't push me."

Jay sat up. In the dim glow Gem couldn't see much of his face; but she could hear the eagerness in his voice, quiet as it was. "But you would?"

"Maybe. Oh Jay, not here. I don't know what's happening." Gem pushed him away, wishing she dared to say yes, please, go on; wishing she wanted to say it. Only, somewhere in the back of her mind was that same feeling she'd had ever since seeing those strange words on the piece of newsprint—that there was something important she was just on the edge of knowing, if only she could remember.

Jay chuckled. "I'll leave it for now. But I hope you'll share a tent at least, because I only brought one."

Without a word, almost hating him though she didn't know why, Gem got to her feet and walked away. When she looked up, she saw the stars. Behind her, Jay was inflating the tent. She was still shivering: It was more than just nerves—she was really cold.

"All ready!" Jay called. Gem ducked into the tent, wriggled into the sleeping tube, and closed her eyes firmly.

The sky was gray outside the tent when she woke. Jay, propped up on one elbow, was looking at her. "Listen," he said. Gem rubbed the sleep out of her eyes. What she had thought was the pulse of her blood in her ears became an external sound. First a whisper, then music. The birds singing to greet the dawn.

Passing for Normal

The rest of the day went by too soon. They spent it on the move, talking, looking, sometimes just listening. "If we get over that ridge there," Jay said at last, "we'll be able to see the tops of the mountains." And then the card in his pocket bleeped.

Jay cursed it roundly and stood still. After a long pause he sighed and said, "Come on. Back we go."

Gem stood looking out into the green plains. "I wish we could stay out."

"They'd pick us up. Massive fines, reporting to Admin daily, the lot." Jay sounded grim; Gem didn't ask if it had happened to someone he knew.

They walked slowly westward. The mono was waiting. They loaded up, climbed in without a word, and sat down. Jay fed the card into the slot. The mono moved off, slowly this time. A bump on the horizon broke its outline and grew into the dull, irregular, crystalline shape that was the City, flecked here and there with green where the rare trees grew. As the sun sank lower in the sky, the shape of the City darkened, and then the sun itself was level with the City rooftops, dazzling them. Jay got up, crouching under the low ceiling of the mono, and sat down facing the other way. After a moment Gem followed suit. They sat with their backs to the City, while the long light of sunset spread across the grasslands.

"That was great, Jay," Gem said as they walked out of the City Edge terminal. "Thanks."

"We'll do it again, I promise." Jay kissed her, as if to seal the promise.

Next morning Gem was struggling to come to grips with some assignments on hologram ethics (Would version-X holograms be an allowable format for the advertisement of livestock?) when an urgent override from the call line flashed up. She let it in.

"Gem—"

"Jay!"

"Can't stop. Parents away till tomorrow, 2 coming up. Be prepared." He closed line, and Gem couldn't raise him again. If she understood correctly, this meant the day exchange between him and J2 was happening. Gem looked at her study quota level. Still low. If she didn't put in at least three hours today, Admin would message her parents, and then all chaos would break loose. Sighing, she swallowed down her impatience and went on with hologram ethics.

As soon as she could, she ran downstairs, only for Ma to call her in for a meal, and after that she couldn't get out of visiting the Store ("Ma, why can't you shop down the line like everyone else?") and going to the sports hall because her exercise quota was down. It was almost evening before she could run through the streets to Jay's house and let herself in.

The screen was up, with the manual control out, so Jay must have set up for J2 to access the data banks. And the food dispenser, Gem thought, looking across the room. And the books.

J2 was lying on his back on Jay's bed, staring through the skylight.

"2?"

He sat bolt upright. "Oh Gem, am I glad to see you. If I hadn't had you to talk to soon, I'd have gone off bang."

"What's the matter?" Gem sat down on the bed beside him.

J2 clenched his fist and brought it down on his right knee. "I'm so *angry*. I wish I hadn't come."

"But—" said Gem.

"No but's," he said. "I'm making myself sick not storming out of the house and shouting at them. *Why did you take this away from me? What had I done?*" J2 banged his knee again, and then his head. "Ow."

"Don't do it if it hurts," Gem said, catching his hand.

"It makes me feel better." J2 unclenched his hand and held Gem's instead. She thought, It's more than this that's hurting him, and I can't stop it. I wish I could.

"I don't know how I shall be pleasant to Jay when he comes back," J2 said.

"He thought he was giving you a treat. Be nice to him."

"Yeah, well." J2 grinned. "After all, he is my brother." He paused, and said, "Besides—I seem to remember it was your idea."

Gem hung her head. "I'm sorry."

"It was a nice thought." J2 stroked the inside of Gem's wrist. "What's this bump?"

"Contraceptive implant," Gem said. "We all get one on our fourteenth birthday." She could hardly feel the touch of his fingers.

"Some present!" J2 stroked it again. "So that's what they look like."

"Don't you have them?"

"Downstream?" J2 turned his wrist palm up. "Not a bump in sight, see? City-controlled issue. Even Kate can't smuggle these down to us." J2 sighed, and his voice slid into bitterness. "Sophie said you asked about Owen Smith. His partner—Fliss Corby—she got pregnant and then lost the baby. It was dreadful."

"It must have been." Gem stumbled among words. "Would the baby have been—"

"It would have been what passes for normal, yes," J2 said savagely, and let go of Gem's hand. "Another girl I heard of, she and the baby both died."

Gem was silent before his anger. J2 sighed again and traced a smile in the air with one finger. "Sorry," he said. "I forget it isn't your fault."

"Sometimes I feel as if it is," Gem said. "I feel as if I could do something, ought to; if only I knew how. If only I knew what would help."

"You don't have to care," J2 said, carefully, almost as if this were a test question.

"Don't you want me to?" Gem glanced up, saw him looking at her, and looked away again. She had seen something like that look in Jay's eyes, the evening they were Outside.

"If I thought you did—" J2 broke off. "I don't know what you want."

"I don't know myself. Yes I do." Gem wrapped her arms around herself. "Jay wants me to—you know—with him." She didn't know what to do: stand up, go away, whatever. Part of her wanted to curl up into a ball and not talk about it. But the rest of her—

"Why don't you, then?" J2 asked.

Gem twisted her fingers together in her lap. Her hands seemed to be the only thing she could move; and then she glanced at J2, leaning on his one elbow. He was watching her hands. She unlaced them in a hurry and sat on them. "Sorry."

"Don't be. Why should you be?"

"Waving my hands in your face."

J2 gave a choke of laughter. "Were you? It didn't look like it to me."

"Don't you *mind*?" Gem said, and then thought, What a thing to ask—who wouldn't mind?

J2 said, very gently, "Gem, this is me. I'm what I was meant to be. Maybe I'm not where I was meant to be, but how could I blame you for that? No more than I could blame you for having a left hand." He took it in his as he spoke. "It's a nice hand too."

They sat there in silence for a while. Then J2 said, "I did ask you a question. You haven't answered it."

"Which question?" Gem said, though she remembered well enough.

"Jay. Why don't you?"

"I'm not sure. I mean, I'm sure there is a reason, only I don't know what it is, except that it's important, unless—" Gem swallowed. "Unless it's because every time I think about him and—that—then I think about you." She stopped. I shouldn't have said that. Too late now.

"Great blue thunderbolts," J2 said. "You can't mean it."

"Do you want me to mean it? Because you— Oh, I don't *know*," Gem said, "but I do care about you. I care."

J2 laughed, very quietly. "So simple," he said. "I'd better go before I forget myself." He hunched up suddenly where he was sitting, as if there were a new pain some-where. "Gem, you do truly mean it? Because if not, say so now and—and put me out of my agony." He laughed shakily.

"No, don't go, I don't want you to go," Gem said. Can I be saying this? she thought. I sound like someone else. "I do mean it."

"Really?" J2 was reaching out his hand and drawing it back again, out and back, as if Gem were hot to the touch and might burn him.

"Yes," Gem said, took his hand and held on. She looked at him. "J2, don't look like that, don't look so—" She stopped, searching through her mind for the right word. He looked as if something wonderful had hap-pened and he was afraid it might be only a dream.

"I don't know what's going on," J2 said in a shaky voice. "For the last twelve years Upstream's been—some-where else, and here it is and here I am, and this is happening. . . ." He turned toward Gem and kissed her, blindly, his hand tight in hers. On the wall the red light began to glimmer.

J2 yawned, stretched luxuriously, and looked up through the skylight. "Gem," he said, "do I dare go outside?"

"Don't ask me."

"Then, if I go outside, will you come with me?"

"Yes," Gem said, "but pray we don't meet anyone."

"*Oh,*" said J2, "I do so want to go out."

"Let's go, then," Gem said, "and never mind praying. I'll find you one of Jay's coats, and keep on your left side."

When they had found a coat, Gem palmed the door open, and they sidled into the night. Under the dark sky a thin rain was falling.

"Wow," Gem said, "it's raining."

"Is that good or bad?"

"Unusual." Gem giggled again. "I'm still high. I can't believe it."

"Neither can I," J2 said, tipping his face up to the sky. "But it is really happening. Apart from anything else, I'm outside, Upstream, I can feel the rain. Gem, I love you."

Gem put her arm around him under the coat. "Come and see where I live."

The rain began to fall more heavily. They walked

across the City, back again. Stopped in dark alleyways—
but all the lights were dim tonight, another energy-saving
drive. And then, on Main Street, a mono slid past them,
all its lights on.

J2 turned abruptly to Gem. "Wasn't that—"

"Yes. They must have come back early."

"You know the way—oh run, Gem, we've got to be
back first!"

"They'll have to check through Center terminal,"
Gem said, but she ran all the same, hearing J2's footsteps
with hers like an echo.

They were only just in time. Gem, standing at the bottom of the stairs down to the basement, had to push J2
through the bedroom door. He backed through, eyes on
something at the top of the stairs: his mother, tall and
black and stately in a wrap that looked like the tropical
fruit counter at the Store, drifting past with her eyes on
something else.

"I knew it was her," J2 said, staring at Gem. "I'd forgotten she was so beautiful." He turned away. "I must go."

"Jay's coat."

J2 shrugged it off. "Will you wait for Jay?"

"No . . . will you tell him?"

J2 shook his head. "Gem," he said urgently, "come
down soon."

Gem nodded. "I will. Look after yourself, J2. Take

care." The ordinary words, the usual ones. Surely she could find something to match this night, that would show J2 how she felt for him? "Soon can't be soon enough," she said.

J2 kissed her and was gone. Gem closed the panel, then ran home through the rain. She set up the Do Not Disturb and tried, and failed, to sleep. In her mind's eye she was following J2 down the slope to the Waterbound territories, across Strand Seven, into the cubbyhole that was his. She lay awake wondering if he was thinking of her, and how soon she could go Downstream again. And whether, if ever, Sophie's plan would work. Whether she would one day see J2 Upstream, by daylight, when all things were open and above ground.

You'll never do it, she heard Jay say in her memory; and to shut out that thought, she rolled over and tried again to sleep.

10

Discoveries

Jay messaged her next day. "Talk about narrow escapes," he said cheerfully. "But did you have a good time?"

Gem's reply was interrupted by an unmistakable giggle. "Who the heck's that?" Jay snapped. "Who's broken in?"

"Who do you think?" the voice said.

"I might have known," Jay said wearily. "If you must bug, Ness, you might do it quietly."

"Well, really," Ness retorted, "if you must do what you seemed to be doing last night, Jay, don't leave it till next day to ask if she enjoyed it."

Something inside Gem turned over with a cold flop, like a wave falling. Jay said, *"What?"* A brief, electric silence. "Is it you or Admin bugging my room, Ness?"

"Both," Ness said. "Good-bye, sweethearts."

Gem heard the breath rasping in Jay's throat. He said, "I'm walking over to your house, Gem. Got that?"

"Yes," Gem said drearily. She closed line and sat down on her bed. J2, I wish I were with you.

Ma let Jay in. He stood with his back to the closed door, tall and angry. "Now," he said quietly, "just what was Ness talking about?"

"It doesn't matter," Gem said.

"It does." Jay backed her up against the wall. "I know I wasn't with anyone, so who were you with?"

"She thought it was you and it wasn't," said Gem desperately. "Just leave it at that."

"If it wasn't me, it should have been," Jay said, putting his hands on Gem's shoulders. "You know I—" He stopped, and Gem felt his fingers digging into her. "I should have known," he said. "It was my brother, wasn't it?" When Gem didn't reply, he shook her. "Wasn't it?"

"Why shouldn't it have been?" Gem said in a strangled voice.

"You know perfectly well why!" Jay said. Then he shrugged his shoulders, letting his hands fall. "Well, after all—why shouldn't you be kind to him? Only I wish you'd warned me."

"It wasn't that," Gem said. "It's more than that."

"More?" Jay put his knuckles to his mouth and stared at Gem. "Just what," he said, "what exactly has been going on?"

"Nothing!—Till last night," Gem said. "Oh, Jay, I never meant to hurt you. And I don't know why it's J2 and me, but it just is. If I could explain it—but I can't— oh Jay—I never thought you'd mind so much."

Jay turned away abruptly, as if she had hit him. "She leaves me for my brother and she expects me not to mind?" he said. "What's he got to give you that I haven't?"

"Nothing, perhaps," Gem said, trying to keep her voice under control. "It makes no difference. As for leaving, was I ever with you?"

Jay ignored the question. "Who do you think you are, Gem Rannesen? Some kind of martyr?" He gave a choking laugh. "That's it. You want the charity kick. I'm a wonderful person, being kind to—to—You think you're going to enjoy it, don't you?"

"That isn't what matters!" Gem took a step forward and put a hand on Jay's sleeve. "Jay, I am sorry, I mean I do sort of wish I could have said yes to you. If I'd never known J2—"

"So it's my fault, is it?" Jay said. "I always was my own worst enemy." His hands moved in an odd throwaway

143

gesture. "Gem," he said, "forget him. There's me. I want you. I love you."

"I don't think I can forget him," Gem said.

Jay pulled his sleeve out of Gem's grasp. "We'll see about that," he said, then shouldered past Gem and ran downstairs. Gem heard her mother opening the door for him.

After the door closed, Ma didn't go back to the family room; instead she climbed the stairs.

"Gemma," she said, "when did you last check your health line? They've messaged me because they set an appointment for this afternoon and you haven't confirmed."

"Sorry, Ma," Gem said automatically. "Will you do it for me?"

Ma went downstairs again. As she reached the bottom step, she said, "Oh, and they said to tell you, it was supposed to be your usual medic but something's happened so it'll be Dr. Avrassian instead."

Well, Gem thought, as straws for drowning girls go, that one will do.

Kate Avrassian looked after most of the City's children at some time or other, so Gem supposed they must have met before, but she couldn't remember. Now, knowing Kate was important, she looked at her as if for the first time. Kate was perhaps in her late thirties, with black hair flecked with gray and cut short. A thin face with high cheekbones, and long eyes under elegant black brows. If she knew that Gem had been Downstream, she was showing no sign of it but moved briskly about Gem with scanners and sensors.

"Nearly done," she said at last with a smile. "Just put your hand under here."

"What is it?" Gem asked, sliding her hand into something that looked like a screen folded inexpertly in half.

"We call it a microx," Kate said. "It checks your blood, skin, or bone—depending which pad I press—by analyzing the chemical makeup for lack of calcium, too much sugar, what you like."

"Too much sugar?" Gem said. "I thought nobody had diabetes now."

"Mostly not. Gene therapy saw to that. And to cystic fibrosis, muscular dystrophy, and most of the other syndromes for which there is a genetic factor." Kate looked at Gem.

"And me?" Gem asked.

"You're as healthy as anything." Kate seemed almost disappointed? Perhaps, Gem thought, I haven't asked the right question.

"And if I fell and broke my neck?"

Kate said, "Provided you didn't kill yourself outright,

we could have you up and walking in three months, maybe less. For which you can thank the scientists who finally managed the trick of regenerating human nerve fiber. Same applies to amputations, accidents, what have you."

Gem took a deep breath and said, "And if I had cerebral palsy?"

The right question. Kate relaxed and said, "I wondered when you'd get around to it. How much do you want to talk?"

"Admin?"

Kate grinned. "Medical confidentiality applies. I can fine them if Bill finds a bug in here—and he'd find anything there was." Kate looked down at the microx. "Sorry. You can take your hand out of there now. Talk away."

"Can you spare the time?"

"I made the time. There was no reason Elli Brunschweig shouldn't have seen you. I wanted to, once Jay Delaiah said you'd found your way Downstream."

"Well," Gem said, "if I had cerebral palsy?"

146

"CP? For a start, you would be either the child of someone who had bought her way out of the tests and hospital, or of someone who managed to duck the system. Under most circumstances we can prevent CP now—monitoring fetal distress to prevent oxygen short-age, catching perinatal jaundice before it sets in." Kate paused. "If J2's mother had had the tests, we could have done a limb transplant *in utero*. The ethics of that is an-other whole kettle of fish." She sighed. "And moreover, you will notice that when I mentioned cystic fibrosis, I said gene therapy and not genetic screening."

Gem frowned. "I don't understand—I thought tests were always done."

"There is a difference. It depends on what you be-lieve."

"What do you believe? What would you do?"

Kate took a deep, not entirely comfortable breath and said, "Therapy but not screening. If we can eliminate the problem, for the person, fine. But for me—not *ever* to eliminate the problem by eliminating the person. Or the potential person. And then, whether you destroy people with CP by making them into people without it—that's another question." She looked straight at Gem and said, "You see, I have the faith that we are all made in the true image. And to destroy or despise the image . . . you don't know what I'm talking about. Never mind. I invited you here for you to talk, not me. Go ahead."

So Gem leaned her elbows on Kate's desk and talked as she hadn't for days. She talked about everything—except that J2 had spent the day Upstream, and what she and he had told each other. Only she did say, "J2 said some of them have babies."

"That's right."

"Are the babies—all right?"

"Yes, when they survive," Kate said. "That is, they're healthy, though rather undernourished, as everyone is Downstream. But they seem to find it harder to cope when they're adolescent. Most that I've known have gone Downstream beyond."

"What is 'beyond'?" Gem asked.

"I don't know any more than anyone else," Kate said. "If anyone does ever send messages back, it's not on a line I can tie into. Anything else?"

"How do you save the babies? How many are there?"

"First question: Again, I can't tell you that. Not that I don't want to, but if you don't know, you can't possibly tell anyone, even accidentally. Second question: Not very many." Kate pushed her hair back from her forehead. "Some I honestly can't save, because it can't be done, or because there's someone breathing down my neck. I hate that. I suppose there are . . ." She paused, thinking. "Ten children in Strand Three at the moment. That is, ten aged twelve or under. And six of those are Downstream born and bred."

"And Mel," Gem said.

"Yes; Mel."

Gem said, "I was talking to J2. We can't understand Mrs. Talmann."

Kate shook her head. "Some things are past understanding. But Bee Talmann had a much older sister with two beautiful babies and everything else she could want. Bee wanted the same. She rushed into marriage—she was only just legal—and then rushed into pregnancy. She wanted everything perfect, and at once." Kate looked at Gem. "For me that would be no reason, and no excuse. But Bee Talmann, poor girl, never had a thought in her head even if she'd taken the time to stop and think it. And she never had another child."

"I think I see," Gem said. There was just one more thing, she thought. "Kate, do you know what Sophie's plan is?"

Kate shook her head. "She doesn't tell me. And we don't offer advice unasked, Bill and I. All I know is that Bill's racking his brains how to get four Ahlfors keys. Sophie's told him what she wants to do, and Ahlfors keys are the only help he can get her."

"Never heard of them," Gem said.

"Me neither." Kate's screen bleeped. She spoke into it briefly and said, "There, that's you cleared."

"Good-bye, then," Gem said.

"Good-bye."

Gem got nearly to the door, stopped, and turned back. "Kate," she said, feeling as if her voice didn't belong to her. She shut her mouth hard.

"What is it?" Kate asked gently.

"Nothing." Now Gem's feet wouldn't obey her. She wanted to leave, but she didn't.

Kate smiled. "Medics always say," she remarked, "that you find out the real problem when the patient's on the way out the door."

"I," Gem said vaguely. She opened the door, shut it again, and almost ran back to Kate's desk. "Kate," she said, "have I got a brother? A sister? Downstream?"

Kate looked down at her own hands: thin, bony hands lying tranquilly on the pale surface of the desk. She wore one ring, an oval black stone set in silver. Gem stepped forward. "Have I?" she asked, her heart thumping hard in her chest. "Kate, I want to know. And anyway—if the answer was no, you would have said by now."

"Her name is Alice," Kate said. "Bethan took care of her. She's six years older than you." She came around the desk and put her hands on Gem's shoulders. "I say 'is,' but I've no proof one way or the other. She went Downstream beyond, two years ago."

"What was wro—" Gem said, the words mechanical between her lips. She mustn't cry. She never did cry in front of people. She mustn't. After a deep breath she tried again. "Why was she sent Downstream in the first place?"

"I don't know," Kate said. "She was never ill in the time I was here, so I never met her, and didn't need to know."

"Tell me some more," Gem said. Her lips felt stiff.

Kate sighed. "Bill met her a couple of times. He said she was a good technician. Bright. Fair hair and a sense of humor."

"Technician?" Gem said. "I'm hopeless at it."

"Sit down, Gem," Kate said. "You're shivering."

"Am I?" Nothing seemed to belong to her. "I ought to go. Pa expects me home for dinner." She moved out from Kate's hands and toward the door. "Thanks for telling me," she said, twitching her lips so that it looked like a smile, and went out.

Gem walked home through the crowded streets without seeing a single thing in front of her. She mustn't break into a run, she mustn't cry. She didn't see Morgan Smith's gaze sharpen on her as she crossed Main Square.

He was still behind her as she palmed herself into the house.

"Gemma?" Ma said when the door rolled shut. "Dinner's ready."

"I'm not hungry." Three steps up the stairs.

"You ought to eat something."

"I feel sick." True enough. Keep climbing.

"Gemma—" Ma came out into the hallway.

"Leave me alone," Gem said. She went into her room, locked the door, the windows, darkened the glass, and switched off the lights. Then for the one and only time in her life, she switched on the faith line. Harmony, it said. Be happy. We are meant to be here. There is a meaning.

Gem lay dry-eyed in the artificial dark, looking up at the ceiling. A tiny red blink of light. The bug detector that Ness had installed for her was busy at last. Admin would be getting an earful of their latest official version of faith.

When the red glimmer of light died, Gem said out loud, "I don't believe a word of it." Whatever it is, it isn't this, it isn't what they say. But something, somewhere. Hidden like the Waterbound. It must be there. Like Alice. Gem rolled over and cried with her face in the pillow, while outside the real night came on, and inside the official version of faith filled the room with phrases.

11

Bets and Bargains

Wen Gem woke up, her chest and throat were still painful from crying, and the room was silent. She crawled off the bed to call Jay, but the screen flashed at her:

Line allocation used until tomorrow

She had heard the faith line switch itself off some time in the black reaches of the night, but had thought nothing of it. Desolately she sat down on the edge of the bed and rubbed her fists in her eyes.

What was there to do? Only work. And where was there to go? Downstream, I must see J2 again, soon, now. She went out into the streets. Drizzle, nothing but gray drizzle. The clouds turned the white walls gray. Nearly all the houses had the insulation skin down over their windows. Gem stood miserably in the middle of the street and got damp.

"What's up with you?"

Even Morgan Smith's voice couldn't make her jump. "Nothing."

"Look, I saw you coming home yesterday. I know something's wrong."

"I don't want to talk about it." Gem shut her eyes as he put his arm around her shoulders. "Go away."

"You and I have got to talk," he said. "And don't worry, I'm not going to revert to the subject of you and me."

Mechanically Gem let him take her to the nearest drinks outlet. They sat down, and Gem leaned her forehead on her hands while Morgan Smith pushed his card into the slot on the table and ordered drinks.

"*Real* coffee?" Gem said a few minutes later.

"Real as I'm here," Morgan said. Gem warmed her hands on the cup but pushed it away. "I can't drink it."

"You're not allergic, are you?" He sounded almost disappointed.

"Trying to buy me over with coffee."

"I'm not buying you!" he snapped. "Give me some credit. Can't I give a girl a drink?"

Gem looked at him. He was in uniform. "Aren't you on duty?"

"You're duty," he said. "Chris Peters put me on to watch you. He's marking Jay Delaiah."

Gem felt her heart chill and shrink to about the size of a hailstone.

"I put a heat-sensitive strip on his skylight," Morgan Smith said. "I check it whenever you call on him." Gem looked at him, and he said irritably, "Oh, I know what you're thinking: Why not look through the glass?"

"Well, why not?" Gem asked, hardly caring.

"Those top-level cats have smart glass, is why. Light in, see out, but no seeing in." Morgan Smith shook his head. "We'll find a way around it one day. Anyway, the heat strip was good enough. Hardly any evidence of two people in that room."

Gem gulped some of the coffee. It burned her mouth but didn't thaw the ice in her heart.

"Since you don't climb out through the skylight," Morgan Smith went on, "where do you go?"

"I'm not telling you."

"You needn't. I went through your printer's memory."

Dully Gem said, "But I wiped it."

"Not thoroughly enough. You're not Ness Brenault." Morgan Smith reached inside his uniform jacket and brought out a folded sheet of paper. On it was printed Gem's map. He showed her, then put it back. "See?"

Gem's coffee cup was empty, he pushed his own across.

"Have mine."

Gem made a confused noise for thank you. "What do you want?" she said.

He looked at her. Uncomfortably, Gem wondered what he would want.

"I haven't told Chris any of this," he said. "No knowledge, no fuss. All I want just now is for you and the Delaiah boy to stop going down there. Then I'll quietly ask someone in Civil to block the tunnels off."

"You can't!" The cry came out before Gem could stop it.

"Why not? There's nothing down there, and it's probably dangerous."

"If there's nothing there, why stop us going?" Sluggishly Gem's brain started to work again.

But Morgan Smith turned the question back on her. "If there's nothing there, why go?"

This couldn't go on. Gem swallowed another mouthful of coffee and asked, carefully. "Do you truly believe there's nothing down there?" She could almost feel him watching her, like a physical pressure.

After a moment he said, "I did, until you said that."

Gem gave a moan of despair and dropped her head on her hands again. Morgan put his hand on her arm, and she jerked back as if he were on fire. "What's down there, Gem?" he asked. "People?" From the tone of his voice she knew he'd meant it as a joke, but she hadn't been able to stop herself jumping again. Incredulously Morgan repeated, "*People?* And you mean, not from the City?"

There didn't seem any reason to answer. She sat quiet, begging her brain to think of something soon, now. Morgan said, "So it really is dangerous. I'll contact Civil."

Gem lifted her head and said, "What about Owen?"

"What?" She could have sworn the pink skin went a shade paler. "I don't know any Owen," he said.

"Your brother."

In the long silence Gem heard Morgan Smith breathing quickly, as if he were a fish gasping for air. "They told us he died," he muttered at last. "He looked dead. Pa took me to the hospital to say good-bye. I touched him. He was cold." Morgan banged his card into the table and ordered another drink. "They told us he was dead, they couldn't save him," he repeated. "I was seven. I had nightmares for weeks. Months."

Gem gritted her teeth and said, "He's not dead. He's alive and I've seen him. So what about him?"

Morgan's drink arrived, alcohol this time. He swallowed it in one gulp. "How did he get there?"

"I'm not telling you. He's not the only one. Other people's brothers," Gem said, and saw him wince.

"Why is he down there?" he asked.

"Same reason as the others. He doesn't match up to

Admin's idea of useful and economic perfection," Gem said savagely, "but for all that he's a living breathing human being like you and me and even Head of Admin."

"All *right!*" said Morgan Smith. "I won't tell anyone. Just stop going there."

"I can't do that."

He turned his head slowly, as if his neck were stiff, and looked at her. "Have you got someone down there?"

"Friends."

He stared and stared at Gem until she had to blink and look down. Then he said, "Why didn't you keep your mouth shut?"

"If you tell anyone, I'll kill you," Gem said.

"You?" Morgan Smith might have been laughing. "You're lucky I haven't hauled you in." He slid down off the high stool. "I wish you hadn't told me," he said bitterly, and walked off.

Gem stayed where she was. There was still some of his coffee left.

"So what's biting you that you don't say hello?"

Can't they leave me alone? she thought. And Ness Brenault is the last person I want to see.

But Ness bounced herself onto the stool and looked set to stay. "Mmm, it's still warm," she said. "Who's been chatting you up?"

"Morgan Smith."

"The dim from Admin?" Ness reached forward. "He's left his card behind—and not coded, silly man." She was wearing blue earrings. The artificial light caught them, blue sparks flying across her shoulders, as she turned her head.

"I ought to take it back," Gem said.

"Never!" Ness said in a long incredulous drawl. "Have a drink on him."

Gem looked at her. "All right," she said, "I will." She took the card from Ness, pushed it in, and selected.

"What about me?" Ness demanded.

"You don't deserve anything. Dropping me in it with Jay."

"True data? How'd I do that?"

Gem stared at her. "Didn't you realize?"

"Realize what?" Ness said, snatching the card as it came back and ordering her own drink.

"I wasn't with Jay."

After a blank look of disbelief Ness shrieked with laughter. "And you were always so virtuous. You!"

"Shut up. Why did you do it?"

"I like breaking into things." Ness drank. "Here's to Morgan Smith and his alcohol allowance, now down to two."

"None," Gem said, "He had one. And I've got the other. Why do you like breaking into things?"

159

"Nobody's got the right to tell me where I can go," Ness said aggressively. "I do it to show them. Break into anywhere, steal anything, that's me."

"Prove it." Gem remembered what Kate had said Sophie needed; she didn't have to think—her mouth did the work for her.

"Why should I?" Ness said, shrugging.

"I bet you," Gem said, and saw Ness's head turn. She was hooked.

"What do you want?" Ness asked.

"Four Ahlfors keys."

"Easy. What's in it for me?"

"Whatever you like," Gem said. "If I've got it."

Ness smiled. "I'll work on it," she said. "Though—"

"What?" Gem said wearily.

"Though," Ness said, "what you might be wanting with one Ahlfors key, let alone four, is beyond me."

"Ask no questions, you'll be told no lies."

"Secretive, aren't we?" Ness mocked.

"When allowed," Gem said bitterly.

"Which reminds me—who were you with?"

"Mind your own data, Ness Brenault," Gem snapped, slid from the seat, and walked off, leaving Ness fingering Morgan Smith's card and smiling.

Well, I blew that one, Gem thought. Ness never did anything yet for me after I snapped at her. Except maybe that once, when she told me to get rid of the map. Gem winced at the thought of the map in Morgan Smith's pocket. I can't go Downstream now; he'll be right behind me. . . .

Where were her feet taking her? She looked around dazedly. She hadn't meant to come to City Edge, least of all City Bridge. But now she was here, she might as well look at the water.

Gem leaned over the edge and looked down. Under the gray sky the water was gray too, sleek as polished stone. What pale light there was came from behind Gem. There was a ghost of the shadow of the bridge on the streambed, a glimmer of her own reflection on the surface. As she watched, another reflection appeared.

"Not thinking of jumping in, are you?"

Gem said, "I thought Morgan Smith was supposed to be shadowing me."

Chris Peters said, "He reported sick. Strange effect you have on him."

"Go away," Gem said.

"I'm on duty. You weren't considering the jump, were you?" Gem looked at him. He was looking away out of the City, toward one of the forbidden zones. How could she find out whether he knew anything at all, without making him suspect her? No way. "Why should I?" she said at last.

"No reason at all," he said.

Since she couldn't make him go away, Gem went away herself; but acutely conscious of him all across the City, like a green shadow in the crowd, his eyes burning on her back.

Despite everything Gem had thought, the Ahlfors keys arrived next day. Ness left them on the doorstep, but at least they were well wrapped. With them was a note:

In return for the day's use of Morgan Smith's card I promise not to tell Admin you asked for these. You still owe me for the things themselves.

Gem sighed, wondered what else Ness was going to want, and slipped the keys into separate pockets. There was no sign of Morgan Smith in the street, but still her heart was thudding as she went to Jay's house. She hadn't seen Jay for two days now. He didn't usually lose his temper for long. Perhaps he would be willing to see things their way—hers and J2's—if she asked.

Jay wasn't there to be asked. Gem took his flashlight and let herself in, through the hole in the wall, down the tunnel.

It was Mike she met first, as usual. "Gem?" said his voice out of the blackness beyond the flashlight.

"How'd you know?"

"I should know the sound of you by now. Jay's with Mel—he brought her some more paper."

"I wanted J2."

"Listen for the singing," Mike said dryly. "He's been insufferably cheerful, ever since he spent that time Upstream."

Smiling to herself, Gem walked down to Strand Seven, and found Sophie before she found anyone else. "Sophie—I've got something for you."

"Oh yes?"

"Kate said you were asking for them," said Gem.

"Really?" Surprise now, and a little less sarcasm. Sophie said, "In that case, let's have some light on it. Come on; Robin's workshop."

Under the light—and very bright it seemed after the usual Downstream dark and dim—Gem fished in her pockets and brought out the four Ahlfors keys.

There was a long, incredulous silence. Gem heard Robin whistle faintly through his teeth.

Sophie said, "Do you ever play cards?"

"No. Why?"

"You have the best poker face I've seen in a long time."

"And a good hand too," Robin said, grinning. He

picked up the keys and turned them over and over as if he couldn't believe in them. "Gem, you're a marvel. How did you get them?"

"I'd rather not say."

"Hmm," said Sophie. "Never mind." She took one of the keys off Robin. "These'll do for us. With these—we'll be flying."

"What are you going to do with them?"

Robin looked at Sophie and said, "I should think we can assume she's on our side?"

Sophie chuckled. "Possibly."

"Oh, for goodness' sake tell me," Gem said. "I'm on your side and I want to know, and I promise in thirty different positions not to tell anyone."

"Then," Robin said, "we're going to take over the sound lines. Talk to you Upstreamers—on our best behavior, of course—so that you can't help but hear. So that there won't be any secrets anymore."

"How?" Gem asked. "With those?" The keys looked very small to be that much help.

Robin nodded. "The thing about the Ahlfors is, not
only can you open any electronic lock, but you can connect up whatever you want power for, and run it from the local source; and you can tap the key into source in all sorts of places. So we can do anything. Anything!" He

grinned again, tossed one of the keys up, and caught it again.

"Where's J2?" Sophie said. "Sal, Theo, Mike? We must tell them. We must plan. Come on!"

Gem said, carefully, "I don't want to cast a blight, but what is so wonderful about now? Why not before?"

"Before, we never had the Ahlfors keys," Sophie said.

Then Robin added, "Besides: Any other time, there were so few people who knew. Easy to keep them quiet somehow. If we can tell the whole City, all at once, which we've never been able to do before, there's no way of keeping it quiet."

The bell for Strand Seven's time at the window sounded. Robin took the Ahlfors keys and put them inside his shirt. "I'm not letting these out of reach," he said.

They went down to the window, meeting Strand Six coming back. The news fizzed and bubbled through the conversations—"On our way!" "Watch us go!" "Not long now, not long . . ." It was like being on a tide of hope.

J2 was at the window before them, looking not out into the day, but back toward the tunnel. Does he know? Gem thought. Is he waiting for me? She dodged past Robin and Sophie and ran toward him. He caught sight of her. "Gem!" A wide grin on his face. "You're wonderful!" He had heard.

"I try my best," Gem said, mock modest, and hugged him. He was warm under the thin pullover. "I've missed you," she said.

"I've missed you." He looked down at her.

"Do the others know?" Gem said tentatively. "About us?"

J2 shook his head. "I didn't like to tell them. Maybe it would seem—maybe it wouldn't be the thing." He sighed. "Let's go and sit by the window."

They sat down, close. Gem felt her skin flutter every time it touched his. With a sick lurch she remembered that Morgan Smith knew she came down here. She hoped—she prayed—he would keep his mouth shut.

"What's the matter, Gem?" J2 asked.

"Why?"

"You shivered."

"Oh, nothing." I ought to warn them, I know that. But I can't spoil it for J2. Not with this buzz of hope through all the Waterbound. Not with Sophie actually smiling at me for once, and Sal signing like windmills. Gem bit her lower lip. I know I don't want to be the one who spoils it. And I'm afraid they'll be angry. I don't want to be here when they find out. I wish I wasn't such a coward. But *please* let the plan work, whatever it really is. *Please.* Careless of whoever might be watching, Gem put her arms around J2. Closer, she thought, as close as we can. Sometime I'll have to leave. Sometime, maybe, I won't be able to be with him ever again. Please, Morgan Smith, keep quiet. Whoever's there, help us. She shivered again, and leaned her head on J2's shoulder.

Fingers tapped her arm. Gem looked up. Sal, hands flickering.

"She says," J2 told her, "nine in the evening, in eight days' time. Listen out—we'll be on the sound lines."

"Ask her," Gem said, "can I come and watch from this side?" She knew enough by now not to offer help. Sal darted off: brief communication with Sophie, back again. Yes, come and watch.

At last the bell rang for the end of window time. Reluctantly, Gem stood up.

"Do you have to go?" J2 said.

"No. Not exactly. But yes, sometime."

"Stay awhile, Gem."

"I shouldn't." But they went to J2's cubbyhole and sat there in the dark, as close to each other as they could get. Gem knew she had to leave, and go on leaving, every time she saw J2. Unless the plan worked. Or unless— Gem stared wide-eyed into the darkness. Unless she stayed down here. Slowly she got to her feet. Don't say anything to J2, not yet. Think about it. "I really do have to go now."

"Yes." J2 sounded sad. "I wish you didn't," he said.

Jay's voice outside. "Tragic, very. Can I come in?"

"Of course," J2 said.

Gem reached for the flashlight and switched it on. There was Jay, standing in the doorway and looking grim. He nodded at J2. "Hi."

"Hi," J2 answered. "You heard the news?"

"Couldn't miss it, could I?" Jay looked at Gem. "Didn't I also hear you saying you had to go?"

"Yes. 'Bye, 2."

"See you soon." J2 kissed her.

"Eight days' time, nine in the evening," Gem assured him, and went out behind Jay. His shadow blotted out the path of the flashlight. All the way up the long slope she watched the light on his back, and he said not a word.

Gem meant to get out as soon as she could. But the minute she stood up after crawling out of the tunnel, Jay took the flashlight from her and threw it down. He grabbed her shoulders and said, pleading, "Gem . . . Gem, don't go down there. Stay with me." He let her go then, and said, "Sorry—I didn't mean to—but Gem, I do want you so much. I do love you. Please believe me."

She could hardly bear the look in his eyes; but she shook her head. "Don't, Jay. Please."

He stood quite still, breathing hard. Then without warning he put his arms tight around her and kissed her. Gem turned her face away and tried to wriggle free. He was much stronger than his brother; she couldn't get away. "Jay, let me go!"

Jay said, "No, I love you, Gem, I told you. You've got to believe me."

With a wrench of her whole body Gem tried to tear herself away. They both fell over. Gem scrambled up faster than she would have believed possible, stamped on Jay's wrist as he reached for her ankle, and ran to the door. There was no sound in her ears except her own footsteps and her own breath; but when she left the house, she heard a crash, as if Jay had hurled something across the room.

Spreading the Word

12

For the next eight days there wasn't a moment when Gem didn't feel sick with tension. She couldn't concentrate on her work; whenever she looked out the window, Morgan Smith was standing there. Once she walked out of the house and around the entire circuit of City Edge as briskly as she could, just to give him something to do. Another time, dragged out to the Store with Ma, she saw Jay across the street, and her heart leaped and thudded inside her rib cage, dreading that he would walk over and take her arm, as if she belonged to him, in a place where she couldn't get away. Jay turned his head and ignored her.

But worse, worst of all, especially at night, was what kept breaking into her thoughts. Alice, sister Alice, where are you now? Couldn't you wait, so I could have met you? And however much she wanted to ask J2 about this, Gem could not: The shadow of Downstream beyond lay across all her questions. It was like birth and bereavement together, finding out about Alice and losing her at once. And, Gem thought, this is what I did to Morgan Smith when I told him about Owen.

Look out the window. Morgan Smith on duty in the drizzle. Did Ma and Pa ever notice that there was an Admin man on permanent fixture in the street? Gem called up a cup of fake coffee from the dispenser—it was all she could afford—and took it down to him.

"What brought this on?" he asked; but he took the cup.

Gem blushed. "I felt bad about—Owen," she said. He shrugged. Gem hovered a moment, shifting her weight from foot to foot. "I had a sister," she said in a quick, quiet voice. "They don't know where she is now, and I never even knew about her, let alone saw her."

Morgan Smith shrugged again. Gem said, "Have you done anything about—you know?"

"No. Not yet." He looked at her. "Go indoors— you're getting damp."

"Will you do anything?"

"I don't *know*," he said, exasperated.

"Please."

He sighed harshly and said, "I can't promise anything. Be careful."

Dispirited, Gem turned away. On the threshold, she turned back. Morgan Smith had called her name.

"Thanks for the coffee," he said.

Almost nine in the evening, eight days later. Autumn had crept up without Gem's noticing it, and already it was nearly dark. She slipped out of the house, moving like quicksilver through the crowds coming back from sports hall. At the corner of the street she looked back. Morgan Smith was still leaning on the wall by the public call line. He must have noticed her, surely? Gem shrugged and walked on.

Jay's parents were on their way out of the house. They smiled vaguely at Gem and said, "Come to see Jay? He's gone out."

"I'll wait for him," Gem said, wondering if they knew anything at all about how Jay passed his time.

Jay's room was in chaos. The bed coverings had been thrown down in a corner. There were clothes on the floor, and other things strewn across the room: as if Jay, usually so meticulous, had turned into someone else. Gem pulled a pile of shirts away from the panel in the wall, and something small clattered to the floor. Gem picked it up. An earring? Jay didn't wear them, but she'd seen this blue glint of stone. She screwed up her eyes in the effort to remember. In Ness Brenault's ear when they were at the drinks outlet.

Gem stared down at the bright thing in her hand. If Jay thought he could get her by making her jealous of Ness, he was on the wrong line entirely. All the same . . . Gem shivered. She put the earring neatly out of the way on a shelf and got down to unclip the panel.

"Is that you, Gem?" J2, not very far away.

"Yes!" Gem said, joy bouncing around her heart like a rubber ball. She closed the panel, ran down; their hands met easily in the dark. "Where are we going?"

"Over the hills and far away," said J2, bubbling over. "No, seriously: up to one of the sound line junctions. Hold on to your hat—I might get lost."

Down into Waterbound territory first: across Strand Three's group room, where the air was electric with talk and the ten children were shrieking at some game in the dark. Up, toward Strand Five: but suddenly J2 turned aside, ducked under a low archway, and said, "Stop a moment, Gem. Anyone there?"

"Mike," said Mike. "Word from Sophie; slow down, there's a delay. All well up there?"

"I've brought Gem. Stand clear!" J2 turned to Gem and said, "There's a hole in the floor, so be careful. We go down it."

Gem sat on the ground and felt for the edge of the hole. "How far down?"

J2 considered. "I can reach the top with my arm stretched. You won't have much of a drop."

"Here I go then." Gem slithered down, yelped as she scraped her front on the edge, and hung on for a second with her feet dangling. The dust slipped under her hands—a small drop, and she was down. A moment later J2 dropped to the ground beside her, staggered, recovered, and said, "Can you see the light?"

"No."

He felt for her shoulders, turned her around, and said, "Over there."

The faintest glimmer, high up, far away. A long climb on an even slope that was almost, but not quite, steep. There was a light running at the top.

"Hi!" It was Robin, in his wheelchair.

"How did you get up here?" said Gem, forgetting to be tactful.

"Friends and willpower, which is what you need in this welded heap of junk." Robin grinned. "Don't knock my brakes off, or you've lost me." He flicked a switch. "Sophie?"

"Here," Sophie said, crackling out of nowhere. "Are the Jays there?"

"Only J2. And Gem."

"Where is the boy? He said he'd be down."

Gem kept quiet. Jay had gone out, his parents said. Could he have forgotten?

"I'll call you again at half past," Sophie said cryptically.

"How are you running it?" Gem whispered.

"Me and my wonderful workshop," Robin said. "And your Ahlfors keys. I told you how they work. At the moment we're tapping City power with them—that's a power line up there—and one of the keys is in an old service slot. At present it's half in, and we can talk to each other on the sound line I've rigged down here. When the key's full in, Sophie can talk to Upstream."

Gem craned her head. Above them, lights: one of the City high-rises. And stars. "We're really close," she said. "Where are we?"

"In an old service shaft," Robin said. "That service slot can't have been used for years. But another thing about the Ahlfors key: It sets off no alarms."

I wonder if Ness knew all this when she took them? thought Gem. She sat down beside J2. The shape of the grating across the dark sky was vaguely familiar. She must have seen it from the other side. After a moment's thought she saw in her mind's eye the places where streets joined. Water channels meeting, and a round hole like a pond.

"That's one of the drains," she said. "If it rains we'll be washed out." Mike giggled.

"Run-through for words," came Sophie's voice out of the black. "Don't put the key full in yet." A pause. Rustle of paper. "Here we go."

Whether it was excitement, or fear, or merely the touch of J2's hand holding hers that stopped Gem from concentrating, she could never remember afterward, but she did remember the end of what Sophie said: "These last words have come down, as a message to us, the Downstreamers. But listen hard: Maybe you will hear the voice speaking to you as well." A deep breath on the air.

" 'You have no need of miracles. You are complete as you are. God gave the fish of the sea fins, and the birds of the air wings. Yet man, who hath not these things, thinks no less of himself. Verily I say unto you, you are not impotent because you are different: you are impotent because you have believed the lies that the world has told you. Your differences are God's gift for the everlasting enrichment of the world. I will cure no one: for I wish not to sow the seeds of discontent: I wish not to sow the seeds of self-hate. Love the light in thyself. That is enough.' "

Sophie's voice, firm, confident, fell silent.

"*That* was all right," Robin said with great satisfaction.

"Good," Sophie said, and Gem heard her draw in a deep breath. "All ready out there?"

"Can you reach the Ahlfors, 2?" Robin said. J2 uncurled from his place on the ground, stood up, reached, and said, "Yes." Gem tipped her head up and looked out through the grating at the lights of the high-rise.

"Go," said Sophie. J2 pushed the Ahlfors key in.

All the lights went out.

Robin and J2 together said something quite unprintable.

"What's wrong?" Mike asked.

"The City's blacked out," J2 said.

"Not just the City," said Robin. "Mike, find me the lead to Sophie if you can."

Noise in the darkness: shuffle, clatter. "Here."

"Thanks." Robin was silent for a few minutes. "Not a squeak," he said bitterly.

Mike giggled again, nervously. "We've blown their generators."

"However could we?" Robin asked. "No, this is something else."

Gem sat in the dark and heard them moving around. J2 laid his hand lightly on her shoulder. "Are we just going to sit and wait?" she said.

"Suit yourself," Robin snapped, as near losing his

temper as she had ever heard him. "*I've* got no option."

"Sorry, Rob."

"Don't apologize," he said. "Either the others are on the lines, or they aren't. Whichever, it won't help if you go scurrying around in the dark."

At the far end of the slope someone called. "Theo," Mike said. His hands touched Gem. "Where's the wall gone?" She heard him pad past and call, "What goes, Theo?"

"Nothing," Theo said, the word blurred on his lips. "Sophie's in a right state."

"Could I have—" Gem said. "I did get the right keys, didn't I?"

"Yes," Robin said. "I tested them up, down, and sideways. They work all right." He sighed. "Pull the key out, J2. I mean, half out."

Gem saw J2's arm move across a distant star, out and back again.

The lights came on. Robin drew in his breath and said, "Shall we try again, Theo?"

"Could do," Theo said. "Yes. Maybe a coincidence."

"Coincidence!" muttered Robin, but he said out loud, "Count of three: one, two, three."

It happened again; and again, and both times the lights came back on when J2 pulled the key half out.

"They *know*," said Robin at last. "They're doing it on purpose. I hope they rot."

"But," said Gem, "how do they know?"

There was a small tearing noise as Robin, clenching his fists on the padded arms of his chair, punched through the cloth with his fingers. He said in a voice that was struggling to stay calm, "Unless they have always known everything we do, which heaven forbid, there is only one way they can have known this. Somebody told them."

"Not me," Gem said. "Cross my heart."

The four of them faced her silently. Even J2 was looking at her, eyes drilling inside her head, searching out lies and untruths and all the dusty corners of her life.

"We believe you," Robin said at last. "Heaven knows why. Which leaves us with two possibilities."

"Kate," Mike said. "Or Bill."

"Jay," said Theo.

"Not Jay," J2 said.

"And Kate wouldn't," Gem said, "surely? Nor Bill. Not after so long." As she spoke she thought, Could Ness—? But she doesn't know what we're doing. Unless Morgan Smith—but he promised he wouldn't tell. Helplessly she sat tight on her thoughts, not daring to speak them aloud.

Robin spoke. "We do have to bear in mind that even if they wouldn't, there are such things as accident and—force."

"They'd never dare," Gem said. "Not Kate. There'd be questions."

"Who knows what Admin might do?—if it is Admin," J2 said.

Robin said suddenly, "I'm slipping." Gem scrambled up and dodged around to the wheelchair. Robin laughed. "No, I meant mentally. We've got the light back, but I haven't tried the sound."

"I've been talking to the other three key holders, that's why," Sophie said. "And then listening to you in case our visiting Upstreamer lets anything drop."

"It wasn't me!" said Gem hotly.

"I'm sure you think it wasn't. But I'll bet you anything you like it was you, somehow," Sophie said bitterly. "Pack up, Rob. Or leave the stuff there, and just bring the key back. We're done for the moment."

"If Mike and Theo will hang on behind me so I don't go splat against the wall at the bottom," Robin said, "I'll be right with you. Can you send some lifters to the hole in the floor by Strand Five?"

"Will do," Sophie said.

J2 said to Robin, "We'll stay here a bit. You may as well

go down in the light. I'll bring the key along when you're through to Strand Five."

Robin nodded. "Okay, boys," he said to Mike and Theo, "brakes off, dragmen on." They moved away. Presently, at the far end of the slope, there was a good deal of laughter and scuffling as Robin was maneuvered up. Someone sang out, "Heave ho!" and someone else, Mike, Gem thought, started a song.

"You wouldn't know they were disappointed," she said.

"We're putting on a show," J2 replied. "For the Up-streamer in our midst. Not that you haven't seen us at our worst already."

"Then why bother?" she asked.

"Who knows?" he said. "Maybe we'll succeed in cheering ourselves up while we're at it."

Mike shouted, "Lights out, 2!" J2 pulled the Ahlfors key out. In the sudden dark Gem heard his feet on the stony floor. She looked up. The lights of the high-rise were fainter now, but the stars were bright. J2 put his arm around her. "Come on," he said. "Back to the glow-worms and howl among the ruins of our dreams."

"Still putting on a show?" Gem said.

"Possibly."

"You don't have to pretend with me, you know."

"No," said J2 in an uneven voice. "I don't, do I?" He rested his head against Gem's. "It's easier in the dark."

"But I don't need to see you," Gem said. "You're in my head. I'm stuck with you."

They kissed each other, then turned and walked down the long slope until they stood below the hole in Strand Five. "If you boost me through," J2 said, "I can haul you up."

They walked back to the group room hand in hand.

"Do we have to go through?" Gem asked.

"Yes," J2 said. "Don't worry, I'm here."

"You don't think it was me, do you? I mean, not on purpose."

"No," J2 said firmly. Then he said, "You mean you may have let something out by accident?"

Gem took a deep breath. "Morgan Smith from Admin knows."

J2 stopped still. "Owen's brother?" he asked, almost casually. And then, "How on *earth* did he find out?"

"My map," Gem said miserably. "He picked it out of my printer's memory somehow. But he did promise he wouldn't tell anyone."

"How long have you known this?" J2 demanded.

"Only just before I last came down. 2, don't tell Sophie, will you? I didn't say anything before—I didn't want to spoil it when you were all so happy."

"Oh, don't try to shield us from life's horrid realities," J2 said. "It only makes it worse when they hit us. All right, I won't tell—unless I have to." He stood still for a moment. "Look, Gem, you must find out whether Morgan Smith told anyone. Or failing that, who fixed the system to react to the Ahlfors key. I don't care how you do it, but *find out*. And then, and then—I still don't know what we do then."

They went into the group room. Under the dim light the white, fierce look on Sophie's face burned into Gem's vision, but all Sophie said was, "Take her away, 2. Then come back and consult."

J2 nodded. "Come along, Gem."

At the beginning of the last slope they clung together fiercely. Gem said, "2, don't ever believe I meant to do it, will you?"

"You shouldn't need to say it again," J2 said. "Don't you trust me?"

"Yes I do, of course I do. But I'm frightened."

J2 said nothing, only held her tighter with his one arm. "Come again soon," he said.

"If I have to fight my way through all Admin," Gem said. One last touch of his hand, and he was gone.

183

13

Waterbound

Jay's room was as empty and untidy as Gem had left it. She could hear someone moving around upstairs: His parents must be back.

Out into the street. There was Morgan Smith.

"You took your time," he said.

"I didn't think you saw me go."

He snorted. "Once I knew you weren't home, there was only one place you could be."

"Why don't you just stick a homer on me," Gem said, "and save yourself the bother?"

"Can't do that; infringes your civil liberties."

"Well I never." Gem hoped she sounded sarcastic enough.

"True! As it is, I'm exercising free will, which I have a right to." He strolled along beside her for a while, and then said, "Did you have anything to do with that little episode of the generators?"

"We thought it was Admin."

Morgan Smith ignored "we" and said, "It wasn't."

Gem felt relief fountaining through her. Admin doesn't know—maybe. "Promise?" she said.

"Promise." He sighed. "I wish I was off duty."

"Why?"

"One, I'm tired of trailing you around. Two, I'm not allowed to kiss you when I'm in uniform."

"Thank goodness for that!"

After a moment he said, "Am I really so repulsive?"

Gem walked on in silence. I could hurt him badly, if I haven't already. At last she said, "There's someone else. And I don't like the uniform."

"I don't always wear it."

"Your mind does," Gem said.

More silence. When they were nearly back at Gem's house, Morgan Smith said, "I do have to tell you something. They're going to put a mesh across the arch at City Bridge. Nothing I said. Someone got hold of the idea that people might fall in."

"You mean they haven't thought of that before?" Gem stopped and stared at him. "You swear you didn't tell them? You swear they don't know?"

"I swear to the first," he said. "I don't know about the

second." He grabbed Gem by the shoulder as she turned away with an impatient snarl. "Gem, I don't know! Who knows how their minds work? They may honestly think someone could fall in."

"What about the other side of the City?" Gem asked. "Where the river comes out?"

"Been fixed for years. A buzzer sounds in Admin if anyone goes closer than—a certain distance."

Gem swallowed. "And does it sound if someone comes the other way, out, downstream?"

He looked blank. "I don't know. Good night, Gem."

Gem went indoors. *I have to think. I really have to think.*

A night's dreaming, a morning's thinking, brought her not much closer to anything other than: *I can't bear to be away from J2. Which means, since the plan failed ...*

Gem closed college line abruptly, halfway through some work on hologram-aided design. *It's no good. I've got to go down to the Waterbound.*

At Jay's house the front door was ajar. She could hear Jay's mother singing somewhere, a rich noise like trickling honey. Gem tiptoed down to Jay's room.

The door wouldn't open. She tried again, smacking her hand into the key plate; again, again until she was just thumping with her clenched fist. At last she ran upstairs and straight out into the street. Around the corner into the next street. There was Jay coming toward her; Ness beside him, their arms draped across each other's shoulders.

"Jay, I tried to get into your room."

Jay said nothing.

"Why couldn't I get in?" Gem asked, trying to sound calm.

"I took your code off."

It was like having swallowed ice cubes. Ness put her arm around Jay's waist. Gem said, "I've got to talk to you, in private. It's important."

"Ness can listen."

"No she can't. This is important."

Ness detached herself from Jay. "Don't worry, Jay. I can guess." She smiled at Gem. "You did say I could have what I wanted. Well, I've got it. And—anyone who can steal an Ahlfors key can set it to cut the source out. Jay asked me, so I did."

Gem's rage got the better of her tongue. "Why don't you just go and jump off City Edge, Ness Brenault?"

Ness laughed and strolled away, pale sunlight glinting on the auburn curls. Gem felt her anger settling at the back of her mouth, sour and miserable. How could Jay do this to her if he loved her? Or to his brother? "Jay, *why* did you do it?"

"Revenge," he said in what might almost have been

the old sarcastic tone of voice, "is sweet. Besides, it's one way of keeping you up here."

She looked at him. Though his face was still and hard, his eyes were like someone else's, trapped and unhappy, trying to get out. Gem put her hands up to her own face for a moment. *I can't argue this out now. I've got to tell him the important thing.* "Jay," she said, "they're going to put a mesh across City Bridge."

"I know. Pa told me. Just as a matter of business."

"Please can I go through your room?" she asked.

Jay shook his head. "They'll have to manage without you," he said. "They always did before." His face was closed, like a door, a screen in an unknown language. "That'll teach you," he said suddenly, viciously.

Gem put the back of her hand to her mouth. "Give my love to J2," she said.

"I'm not going down anymore."

"What?"

"You heard."

Gem was going to ask, *Why not—don't you care anymore? What went wrong?* Another look at Jay's face told her it would be no use. He wasn't even looking at her. "Jay," she said, "I never thought I'd wish you hadn't met me."

He flinched and glanced at her. "When I met Alice,"

he said, turning away again, "I wanted to find out what you were like. I asked Kate how to find you."

"And the same with Ness, because of Sal?" Gem said, unable to think of anything else. There was no reply; Jay walked off after Ness without looking back.

Walk. Keep walking. Maybe it'll help me think. Mechanically Gem moved her feet. The houses slid past, and all her brain could come up with was: Three options open now. One, to accept the situation. Two, to go down through Kate Avrassian's tunnel in the hospital. Three—her brain shied away from option three. Let's not think about that yet. Presently she looked up. I've been walking for hours. In circles. Which way to the hospital?

In Recep Hall the first person she saw was Chris Peters, standing by the doorway that led to, among other things, Kate's office. He saw her as she came in, and looked beyond her. Gem turned around—yes, there was Morgan Smith, still outside.

"What are you doing here?" she said to Chris Peters.

"On my usual duty."

"Where's Jay, then?"

"In Minor Cas." Chris Peters looked at her quizzically. "He came in before, just over a week ago, with a cracked bone on his wrist. Said somebody stamped on him, but he wouldn't press a charge or say who."

Gem went out again before he could ask why she was there.

Home, upstairs, the call line had a message recorded.

"I don't seem to be able to find you," Pa's voice said, "so perhaps you'll answer this message by coming downstairs. Your mother and I want to talk to you."

"Oh no," Gem said aloud, "what now?" She sat down on the bed. Do I do this now and get it over with, or wait till I feel more like it?

Do it now. She went downstairs.

"I got your message."

Pa looked around from his work screen. Ma had her reader line on private—she was probably listening to some romance or other; but when Pa stood up, she switched off and sat looking at the air between him and Gem.

"I'm glad you condescend to notice us, Gemma," he said dryly. "I have had a message from the college line. Not only has the standard of your work dropped sharply, but you are a long way below quota."

"I'm sorry," said Gem, not managing to suppress a shrug. What did that matter, beside everything else?

"Pray don't be so casual about it," Pa said. "I have no wish to be demoted a level because my only child is not making her full contribution to society."

"Liar," Gem said.

"I *beg* your pardon?" Pa said coldly. His face had gone quite white.

"I'm not your only child."

The silence was intense. She waited for them to say something; they said nothing.

"Why did you never tell me about Alice?" They looked blank, and Gem said furiously, "All right then, your other daughter!"

"More to the point," Pa said, his voice clipped as if he were trying to keep it in order, "how did you find out?"

"That is not the point," said Gem, coldness matching coldness. "However I know, *I know*; and I had a right to know before."

Ma looked up and said, "But it was so long ago. You could never have known her, whatever we told you."

Gem said, "She was still alive two years ago."

Ma gasped, but Pa's face merely took on a tighter, more closed look. "How can you possibly know that?" he demanded in a quiet, harsh voice.

"I have been told." Gem put her chin up.

Pa stepped forward. "Tell me you're lying, and maybe I'll forgive you," he said.

Gem looked at him. "Why should I lie? I have nothing to hide."

"Gemma," her mother said pleadingly.

"How could you do it?" Gem asked. "Live as if she

never existed? Never tell me, when I always wished I had a sister?"

"Gem," her mother cried, "what else could we do? The hospital told us she was dead. We went to see her, and—I was so sure she was dead. They said she would never have had a real life anyway—there was something wrong with her." Ma put her hands up to her face briefly, and said, "They told us we should think of her death as a blessing. And then you were born, and you looked just like she did when you were a baby. So do you think it was *easy* having you, wondering all the time what *she* might have been?" Ma stood up and went to stand beside Pa. "Who called her Alice?" she asked.

"I don't know. I thought you did."

Ma shook her head. "I could never think of a name for her—she was just my little girl—but where has she been? How do you know, however do you know, what have you been *doing*?" Ma broke off and stood trembling. "I'd never have had you if I'd known you would hurt me like this!" She buried her face in Pa's shoulder, and slowly he put his arms around her.

Gem whirled around and ran out of the house. She did not want to think of them. She had a sudden, nightmare vision of losing J2, his hand slipping through her grip, of losing Alice the same way.

I can't bear it. Option one, never. Option two, no

good. Option three; time to think about option three.

The Store was open. She used all her remaining credit to buy a solar flashlight like Jay's, a key for Outside, a length of strong cord, a waterproof sack, and some chocolate. In her room again she wrapped the hard things in clothes and pushed them into the sack. As much paper as the printer would give her. A bright idea: She keyed her food intake data into her health line and was promptly issued food supplement pills. *I knew I wasn't eating enough.* Last, the ceramic tray full of the grass she had grown from seed picked on the second day Outside with Jay. She slung the cord from one shoulder.

Now, quietly. Downstairs. She could hear her parents talking together. At the sound of their voices she felt her fists curling up. *I'll miss them later. But not now.*

At City Gate she fed the key into the slot. It was spat out again, one side bright red. She had been gated.

Gem leaned against the fence and tried desperately not to cry. *I climbed out once before. I can do it again.* She opened her eyes. There was Morgan Smith.

"Where were you going?" he asked.

She looked at him. "Let me out, Morgan."

"I daren't."

"I'll climb over if you don't." A long pause. "Look," Gem said, "do this one thing for me and I'll never bother Admin again." Still he hesitated. "Morgan, *please!*"

"I can't believe I'm doing this," Morgan Smith said; but slowly he reached out to City Gate. "There you are. Go on, and be quick about it."

"Thanks," Gem said. "Good-bye." She slipped through the gate. Don't look back. Quick, alongside the stream till you're under the bridge. No mesh yet, but a single metal bar like a stalactite under the arch. Gem doubled the cord, wrapped the loop around the bar, and fed the loose ends through the loop. The water curled around her ankles. There was nothing to stop the loop slipping off the end of the bar. Gem pushed it as high as she could reach. Pray it doesn't slip off till I'm down. Quick, quick. She turned, knelt, and, facing out through the arch of City Bridge, slithered down, following the stream under the City.

Down into the wet tumbling darkness, like jumping off the edge of sleep into a nightmare. Gem turned her face aside out of the water and slowly, with her hands twisted in the cord, let herself down. After what seemed a lifetime, she knew from the sound of the water that she was near the bottom. But then the loop slipped off the end of the bar.

She fell about a meter and landed on her back in the stream, cushioned by the sack of clothes. The cord landed stinging across her face. At least that means there's nothing to show which way I went. She staggered to her feet, bundled the cord into an awkward coil, and set off. *If I keep on downstream, I'll find the jetty.*

"Where did you spring from?" Sophie said a while later, and then, "Don't tell me, I can guess. You're soaked."

"Yes." Gem felt tremendously tired. She could hardly lift her hand to wave hello to Sal, who was standing behind Sophie's wheelchair.

"So what hindered you from coming the usual way?" Sophie asked.

I daren't tell her. I can't.

Sal stepped forward and signed something with an emphatic flick and smack of her hands.

"Sal says," Sophie translated, "did you find out about the power cut?"

The habit of truth had too strong a grip on Gem for her to duck the question. "Ness Brenault did it. Because Jay asked her to."

There was a long, icy pause. "I thought I hadn't seen much of him lately," Sophie said in a flat voice. "And so why did he ask her?" She looked at her hands as if they didn't belong to her and began signing to Sal. When she stopped, Sal made a gesture like wringing necks and walked off with a set face.

"You heard me," Sophie said. "Why did he do it?"

"I think because of me . . . and J2. I didn't ask him that. He did say that he's not coming down again."

"I wish," Sophie said, and drew in a ragged, hissing breath, "I wish you'd never come here, Gem Rannesen."

Gem shivered in her wet clothes. "I'm sorry. Were you and J2 ever . . . well—oh, you know what I mean to say."

"The answer is no," Sophie said. "I wanted Jay, if you must know, not that it does either of us any good, and what I get is you, swanning around showing off your legs and most of the rest besides."

Gem ducked her head. "I won't argue with you."

"Don't make allowances for me," Sophie said. "Argue. Go on. You've got the best of both worlds, you have, and because you can't get what you want Upstream, you come here to play Madame Bountiful." Sophie was spitting the words out. "You want me to be grateful for your kindness? I am not. Don't think I'm pleased because I smile. Don't think we're any of us contented to be here because here we stay. Don't think at all if you can help it; then maybe we can get on with our own lives instead of

clearing up the mess you make."

"Do I have to be stupid," Gem said loudly, "because I'm from Upstream? I don't *care* whether you're grateful or not. I like you, I don't know why, considering you never open your mouth without getting at me. Can't a girl come and see her friends?" She blundered past the wheelchair. "I want J2."

He wasn't in his cubbyhole. Gem stripped and put on some dry clothes. She took out the tray of grass. Some of the earth had fallen out, but the tangled roots were holding the rest together. Perhaps they would let her plant it near the window. She lay down with her head on the sack for a pillow.

After a time, long or short she did not know, Gem woke from a doze to find J2 sitting beside her. "Sophie told me who fixed the power cut," he said. "Is it true?"

"Yes." Gem reached for her new flashlight and switched it on dim.

"I don't believe it." He sat for a long time hunched up, his arm across his chest and gripping his left shoulder. At last he said, "Jay said to me once he told you how I came here. And why Ma wasn't found out before."

"Because you had a twin who died."

He nodded. "What he doesn't know is that when he was born, I felt as if he was the twin, come back. I really did. And now—I can't believe he's done this to me, I can't. Why did he do it?" He looked at her. "Did he tell you?"

"Not exactly," Gem said. "But when he found out about us . . . because he wanted me himself. I think that was why."

"He never said anything to me." J2 looked at Gem. "Nor did you."

"I hoped he might understand."

J2 shook his head. "He always did go into a raging fury when we were small, if I had something he didn't." He hunched up tighter. "Gem, you shouldn't have come down here."

"But I had to," Gem said. "I want to stay." She sat up, moved close to J2, and began loosing his fingers from their tight grip. "I told Jay we love each other. For my part, I wasn't lying."

J2 let Gem take his hand and put hers against it, palm to palm, fingers spread. "How will you go back? I suppose Kate will let you through."

"Didn't you hear me?" Gem said. "I'm staying."

"You can't."

"What's to stop me?"

"But Gem," J2 said, words suddenly tumbling over each other in the urgency of his speech, "how can you give up everything you've got, your parents, education, everything you could have that I'd *kill* to get. How can you?"

"I don't know!" Gem cried. "I just know I'd rather be here."

J2 let out a long, shaky sigh and slipped his hand

around to hold Gem's wrist. "And I'd rather have you here. Just don't go changing your mind, that's all."

They spent that night and a lot of the next day curled up in J2's cubbyhole, not doing anything in particular, only being together. Toward what might have been late afternoon J2 said, "Gem—I want to go up to Jay's room. Just in case."

"In case of what?" Gem said. They looked at each other. "Oh, all right," she said.

Gem had lost count, now, of the times she had walked this way, but after a while she said, "I never thought it was so far."

"We're on the right path," J2 said. "There are your footprints."

And Jay's, Gem thought, but he doesn't say that. They began the long climb up the last of the tunnel.

"Gem," J2 whispered, "there's a light. His panel must be open."

"But he said—"

"I know he said." J2 stopped walking. "He always has been one for the dramatic gesture."

"This wasn't any gesture." Gem stopped too, her shoulder against his. "I suppose it might not be Jay."

"Who, then?"

"Only one way to find out." Gem hitched her jacket

forward. "You stay there. I'm more likely to know who it is." She walked on again. Despite what she had said, J2 followed her; she could hear him. He stopped just outside the light, and Gem went forward into Jay's room.

More Flowers

J ay was not there. In the corner farthest from the tunnel entrance, cross-legged, her hair strained back and tied with a piece of string, sat Ness Brenault.

"You!" Gem said.

"Hi, Gem." Ness tossed something from one hand to the other.

"How did you get here?"

"I meant to see what you and Jay've been up to." Ness tipped her head back and smiled slightly. "But I don't like the dark."

"But how did you get the door open, and anyway where is Jay?"

"Jay is cooling his soul in the wind and the weather," Ness said. "And you forget the way I am." She held out an Ahlfors key. "I took one for myself."

Gem stared at her. "Wait a moment." She backed down the tunnel again toward J2.

"It's not Jay, is it?" he said. "I can hear that much."

"Ness Brenault," Gem said. "Come to see what all the fuss is, and afraid of the dark."

J2 grunted. He turned toward the streak of light across the wall and rubbed it, as if it might come off on his hand. "May as well show her," he said, and went forward.

Gem followed into Jay's room. When she came through, he was already on his feet and looking down at Ness. "I'm Jay's brother," he said. "Do my parents know you're here?"

Ness said, "I took good care Jay's parents would be out. Was it you with Gem, that time?"

"It was. Are you coming down? I gather you want to see the show."

Ness said lightly, "Who am I to turn down a new experience? Lead the way." She got to her feet and flinched, as if she had only just noticed J2's left shoulder. "What's it like down there?" she asked.

"I can't tell you what it's like—I've hardly been anywhere else. I can tell you what it is."

"Well?" Ness said.

"Cool and dark and rather damp, except by the windows."

"Sounds dire." Ness took a hesitant step toward the tunnel. "Windows?"

"One or two. Not where you'd see them from outside." J2 waited, to let Ness go first. She did not move. "Do you like it down there?" she asked.

"What have I got to compare it with?" J2 said acidly. "I don't like not existing, I can tell you that. Because I don't exist, do I? You didn't know about any of us. Who does?"

"Someone must," Ness said defensively.

"They're taking good care not to tell. But I'm here, or down there, or wherever. And you've got all this"—for the first time J2 moved, a sharp outward gesture of his hand—"and now Jay, as well. How greedy can you get?"

Ness's eyes glittered. "Let me tell you, I didn't take Jay. He came running. As for greed—how else do you get what you want?" Ness's usual insouciance had deserted her. She stood rigid, her fists clenched and her nails digging into her palms. "Well," she said, "I'm not having either of you call me a coward," and got down to crawl into the tunnel.

Gem followed her. "Where's Mike?" she said, a little while after the tunnel leveled out.

"Not scouting. What's the use?" J2 replied. They came to the group room in the dark, except for the crack of light that shone out where Mel's door was just ajar.

"Can't we go in there?" Ness said. "I could do with seeing my hand in front of my face."

J2 knocked. "Mel, can we come in?"

A soft answer from Mel. J2 opened the door, and the light spilled out. Mel was sitting with Jay's old lamp on the table in front of her and the tide of folded paper flowers around her feet.

"Let's do one, Mel," Gem said. She had been down there so often now that she no longer needed showing how to fold flowers with Mel.

"This is Melanie Talmann," J2 said. "Mel, this is Ness Brenault."

"Does she do this all the time?" Ness asked, watching Mel start on another flower.

"Yes."

"She's crazy."

Mel's hands froze for a moment; then she went on with the flower. Gem finished the one she was folding, added it to the pile, and hugged Mel. They went out. J2 shouted, "Mike!"

A sound of footsteps. "Here."

"Run and ask Rob if there's enough power for us to have the glowworms awhile, please," J2 said.

"Will do." Mike ran off.

"I can't see a thing," Ness said. "How can he run?"

Gem said, "He can't see either—he's blind. But he knows the way."

There was a long wait before the glowworms came on. In the dark Gem heard Ness fidgeting, and her breath coming fast.

J2 began to do the honors stiffly, as if at an exhibition. Mike came back, was introduced, nodded, and turned away. Sophie stared coolly at Ness, said, "So you're the one," and looked down at the cord she had been braiding in the dark.

"And this is Sal," J2 said. Sal's hands flickered in a question. J2 replied, and Sal stared at Ness with an intent, hungry look. He's told her who Ness is, Gem thought. Is he going to tell Ness that Sal's her sister?

Sal smiled at Ness. Ness stared back blankly. "What's wrong with her?" she said.

"Nothing," J2 said. Still Ness stared. With an abrupt movement of her hands, Sal turned aside and ran out of the group room into one of the tunnels. They heard her footsteps die away.

J2 looked at Ness. "What would you like to see now?"

There was no answer.

"Had enough?" Gem said.

"Yes," Ness answered, and then again, "Yes, take me back, Gem, quick." She didn't say good-bye to the others, didn't speak a word on the way back. When she wriggled across the threshold into Jay's room, it was with a sigh of relief.

" 'Bye, Ness," Gem said.

Ness turned back and said, "Spare a moment, Gem?"

"All right." Gem stayed where she was.

"Oh, come in and sit down," Ness said. "I can't talk to you like this."

Gem went in and sat on the edge of the bed. Ness sat down beside her, turning the Ahlfors key over and over in her hands.

"Gem," she said, "you're not going back there?"

"Yes."

"How can you?" Ness looked sideways at her. "In the dark all the time. With people like that."

"Like what?" Gem said, keeping her voice flat.

"Well—that brother of Jay's."

"We love each other."

Ness stared at her. "But—" She shook her head. "I don't understand you, Gem Rannesen."

"More's the pity," Gem said. She stood up and went back to the tunnel mouth. As she went, she kicked against something: a paintbrush in a jar of cleaner. Gem turned the panel to see what Jay had been painting. It was deep pitch-black, not yet dry. She turned it back. "Shut the panel behind me," she said.

Gem stumbled down to the group room in the dark. There was J2. She put her arms around him and held tight.

If Gem had ever wondered how the Waterbound filled their days, she found out now. There was silence only during the times at the window, when people could see to read, sew, mend. Otherwise there was more talking than she had ever heard in her life: storytelling, singing, the history of the Waterbound Downstream told and re-told and reaffirmed. Gem found she could remember some of the protest songs from her project; the Water-bound fell on them avidly, and Gem sang herself hoarse.

> *If living were a thing that money could buy,*
> *Then the rich would live, and the poor die.*
> *All my trials, Lord, soon be over.*

"That should go in one of the encyclopedias," J2 said. "Come on."

By the light of Gem's flashlight Sophie was pinning up more facts and opinions. Bill had run the gauntlet of all the detectors to smuggle some more bits of books from Recycling to Kate's office in his repair kit. J2 scribbled down the new quotation with a stub of graphite and put it in front of Sophie.

Gem read from the wall. " 'The corn was Orient and Immortal wheat.' Why that one?"

"I like the sound of it."

She read again. " 'Then shall the lame man leap as an hart, and the tongue of the dumb sing.' "

"I wish he would. I wish I could."

Tentatively Gem said, "But then you wouldn't be you."

"No," Sophie said bitterly, "I'd be Upstream, wouldn't I? The City could stop being afraid of me." She tacked the new opinion down harder than she needed. "There's no cure for being like me. There might be a cure for plain straightforward cowardice." Sophie sat still for a moment. Then she said, "Buzz off, both of you. You don't know how lucky you are."

Gem slipped her hand into J2's. He said, "Where shall we go?"

"Let's go and sit with Mel," Gem said. "I feel I need soothing."

As they approached Mel's door, J2 bent and picked something up. "She's dropped one of her flowers."

Gem looked into the room, took a step forward. Drifts

of paper flowers rustled around her ankles. "Mel! Melanie!" The table was covered with squares of paper, all sizes. Mel had been making the flowers smaller and smaller: There was one hardly bigger than Gem's thumbnail. Gem went out. "J2, she's not there."

Neither was J2, but in a moment he came back, his face curiously blank in the dim light. "She's not there," Gem said again.

"No," J2 said. "You can see her footprints. She went down to the water."

"Can she swim?" Gem asked, and then realized what he was saying. "She can't have gone Downstream beyond!"

"I think she has." J2 swallowed and said, "I suppose it is just possible she's only walking by the river." They went quickly, in silence, out of the strands, into the edge of the sunlight shining in where the river came out from under the City. Before them were Mel's small, neat footprints. They led straight into the water. J2 ranged grimly along the shore, looking for them to come out.

"*Can* she swim?" Gem asked again.

"I think so." J2 was still holding the flower he had picked up, a pink one. He set it down on the water. It drifted, spun, and suddenly was swept downstream, toward the sunlight. "She's gone, whatever," he said.

There was still some chance that Mel was elsewhere with the Waterbound. Word was sent around, but reply came back fast: No, Melanie Talmann's not with us.

That evening, instead of gathering in the group room,

Strand Seven went down to the window. Gem sat apart. They won't want me. A single candle was burning in the center of the group.

Someone came in. Gem didn't recognize him, didn't think she'd ever met him.

"Is it true?" he said.

"It's true." Sophie lit another candle from the one in front of her. "Ask Strand Five to burn this for her, Nick."

"Sure." It was put into his hands. Nick, walking slowly, left them.

Sophie said, "The names of those who have gone Downstream beyond," and Gem saw that she was reading from a book. As she spoke, Robin signed her words to Sal, who was sitting curled up beside his wheelchair.

It was a long list. Gem heard the names of Ken and Gina that she had seen written in the cement, but the rest were strange to her, until the end. "Alice Rannesen," Sophie read, "Tom Burke, John Hendriks, and Melanie Talmann. Waterbound no longer."

She closed the book. There was a long silence, and the candle flame wavered in the shadows. A woman Gem had never seen before walked in, an awkward lurching walk not unlike Theo's. "Annie Dasilva, Strand Two," she said, and held out a candle. Sophie lit it from her own. Someone else came in and lit candles for Strands One and

Three; two people together for Strand Four. Strand Six, Strand Eight.

"That's it," Sophie said. There was another silence.

At last Theo spoke. "What," he said, "what do we do with the flowers?"

A flicker of movement: Robin's hands, translating for Sal. Then Sal clapped her own hands, so that everyone looked at her, and then she signed at them.

"Sal says," Robin said, "that we ought to send Mel's flowers after her on the water."

"Won't they go soggy?" J2 asked.

"Wax them," Sophie said.

"What with?"

"Melt some of the candles down."

"We've not got many," Robin said.

"This is more important. Tell Sal yes, Rob," Sophie said, but signing as she spoke.

A pause. "Sal says we could write messages on them," said Robin.

"What sort of messages?" Mike asked, and the others took it up without waiting for a reply.

"Save our sanity."

"Send chocolate!"

"Help help I am trapped in a lower reality." That was Sophie.

"Send us the key!"

Half a dozen other suggestions, until Robin laughed and shook his hands. "I'm getting signer's cramp. Has anyone any *real* ideas?"

J2 said slowly, "Why not do what we were going to do with the sound lines? Tell them about us."

"That's a good one," Sophie said.

Gem ventured to speak at last. "There are an awful lot of flowers."

"There are all the Waterbound," Sophie replied. "Mike, will you scout around and spread the word?"

"Sure," Mike said.

"Don't take all night," Theo told him, and Mike loped off.

Robin said, "Robin's wonderful workshop will now figure out some way to wax paper," and wheeled himself out.

Hours later. "I make that two thousand," J2 said. "Give or take a handful."

"We can't write on the smallest ones," Sophie said. "We'll just float them off. That leaves a dozen or so for every one of the Waterbound to write on. How's the waxing?"

"Fast and furious, Rob says." J2 laughed. The air was almost lively again, the way it had been when Gem had brought the Ahlfors keys down.

Mike appeared behind Sophie's chair. "Rob says we'll be up all night if we start writing now."

"We'll do it tomorrow, then, and take them around the other strands," Sophie said. "Isn't it way past time to eat?"

"I'll have a look at the nets," J2 said. "And Nick said they could spare some mushrooms from Strand Five."

There were fish in the nets, and barely enough power to cook them; Gem wondered if the Waterbound ever had enough food. She had to resist the temptation to ask for more. She had given her food supplement pills to Sal, who was cook, the day she came down, but she was still uncomfortably aware that feeding her was an added drain on the Waterbound resources. Now she took some of the precious chocolate from her bag and shared it around.

Mike licked chocolate from his fingers. "I could get used to this stuff," he said in a voice of deep contentment. There was a laugh.

"True," Sophie said. "But bring some more vitamins next time, Gem."

"What next time?"

"Too right," Sophie said. "There won't be one."

They spent the morning of the next day writing, or carrying paper flowers to the other strands, and heaping them at the water's edge. Mel's footprints were still there, blurred now, disappearing into the sand. Strand Seven stood looking at them.

"It seems we start the flotilla," Sophie said.

"You first," said J2.

"No, Sal first—it was her idea."

Sal waded out and set her flower carefully, very carefully down on the surface of the water. It caught the current as she stepped back, and was whirled away downstream almost faster than they could watch. As it disappeared, Gem heard a sigh go up from the group at the edge of the water. There were others standing behind them, a silent crowd stretched back through the dimness into the dark, all the Waterbound.

Sal splashed ashore laughing and took Robin's hand. With a smile Sophie tossed her own flower onto the water and watched it go. Robin, Theo, Mike, J2, then the rest of them pressed forward.

"Come on, Gem," J2 said. "There's hundreds of these to get floating. We haven't got all day."

"Yes we have," said Sophie. "But I must say there's no point in waiting. Go on, Gem."

"But should I?" Gem asked.

"You're down here, aren't you?" J2 said. "What does that make you if not one of us?"

"Reckless and quixotic is the answer," Sophie said. "It's all right, Gem, join in; come and help."

The Unbinding Begins

Gem uncurled from her sleep at J2's side and sat up. There was someone standing near them. She groped for the flashlight and switched it on; the light moved upward, onto a face.

"Jay!" she said, very softly.

"Hello, Gem." He sat down on his heels.

"What are you doing here?"

"I changed my mind."

"You might have changed it sooner," she said bitterly.

"I might not have changed it at all," Jay replied. "I suppose I would have been sorry in the end."

"And you're sorry now?"

"I hate myself," he said. "Satisfied?"

"Don't be a fool, Jay." It was J2. He had woken up unnoticed. "We all do stupid things sometimes."

There was a small silence. Then Jay asked, "Whose idea was it to send the flowers down?"

"Sal's."

"You picked your day for it," Jay said. "First real sunshine for weeks, and half the City out enjoying it." He turned to Gem. "You know that sandbank about a kilometer down? Lots of them came aground there. People were unfolding them and reading the messages."

"And saying something ought to be done?" Gem asked.

"Not that I heard." He shook his head. "No. It was strange, watching them, once I realized what had happened." Jay smiled. "Trust you to hit the spot, 2. I heard someone say, '*Jon* Delaiah? Surely not?' Then she marched off toward Pa with the paper in her hand. . . . He looked very strange when we got home."

"So I should hope," J2 said. "Meanwhile, isn't it the middle of the night?"

"I came down because I couldn't sleep," Jay said. "May I use some of your floor?"

"Stay, and welcome," J2 told him.

They awoke in what was probably next morning, but might have been the Arctic winter for all they could see of it. There was a strange, blank feeling in Strand Seven: the message sent, the thing done, what now? They waited hungrily for their time at the window, and when the time was rung they went without a word.

Never since her first journey down Jay's tunnel had Gem known it so quiet. When they reached the window and the lines of plants, she let the others crowd against the glass. Theo put both hands as nearly flat against it as he could manage and leaned there like someone trying to break down a door. Mel's absence was among them all, in the words they didn't say.

Gem backed away from the group. Even J2 was up by the window with the rest, his hand in a patch of sunlight on the dusty floor. And where was Jay? He had started off behind them on the way down. Perhaps he couldn't face meeting them all. And then, with a thump of her heart, she remembered that Jay wouldn't know about Mel. He would have gone to see her as usual.

Gem's feet took her away from the window before she could think. They thudded through the dark, running blind. She knew the way, without light, without help, for the first time. "Jay? Are you there?"

The room was dark, the tide of flowers gone. Jay came in behind her from one of the other tunnels, carrying his flashlight. "Gem—" He saw her face in the flashlight as she turned around, and stepped back. "Where is she?"

"Jay, she— I'm sorry, we never thought to tell you before—she went Downstream beyond." Gem closed her eyes. She couldn't bear to see the look on Jay's face. "That was why we sent the flowers," she said.

"I see." Jay's voice was hoarse. He rubbed his eyes. "Ness said she came down here, is that right?"

"Yes. We found her in your room."

"She told me. She hated it here." Jay banged his fist on the wall. "If it was her that upset Mel, I'll kill her."

"And then what would you tell Sal?" Gem asked.

"I know, I know . . ." Jay sat down on the floor, head bowed. "I make such a mess of things," he said. "Me and my filthy temper. Can you forgive me, Gem?"

"It's not me you should be asking, but yes." Gem sat down beside him. "Did you tell Ness you were coming here?"

"No . . . she was telling me how disgusting it all was, and suddenly it developed into a screaming row, and then I told her Sal was her sister, at which point she banged out of the room and I realized I was defending every-one." Jay laughed shakily. "Perhaps I should stay down here for good."

"I'm going to."

He looked at her seriously. "I had a call from your ma. You ought to go back."

"With J2 or not at all."

"Oh." He was silent for a while. "Did they read the lists for Mel?"

"Yes."

Jay bowed his head again. "I wish—but it's no good now."

"Come down to the window," Gem said.

"Sophie—"

"What about Sophie?"

"She doesn't know I've come back yet." Jay looked at Gem. "I suppose you told her it was Ness and me."

He was losing all his old precision of speech. Gem said, "She asked me if I'd found out anything about the power cut. I couldn't say I didn't know."

Jay said, "Would you have told her if she hadn't asked?"

"It's a big if," Gem said. "I think I'd have kept quiet; for J2's sake. I don't know."

Jay stared at her, then got to his feet. "Let's get it over with," he said.

When they came down to the window, Jay didn't hesitate but walked straight to Sophie's chair and knelt down beside it. "Sophie," he said, "I'm sorry."

"So J2 tells me," Sophie said, not unkindly. Her face was turned aside: Gem couldn't read it.

"What can I do?" Jay said.

"There's nothing to be done." Tentatively Sophie laid one hand against Jay's face. "Call it a clean slate," she said.

"Less trouble all around."

Jay sat back on his heels. The air seemed to clear; but there was still the sense of something not done. Suddenly Mike said, "What now? I can't stand much more of this— what do we do now? How can we just keep *waiting*?"

"You're right," Sophie said. "Let's go."

"Where?" J2 said.

"Downstream. Beyond."

Someone gasped, someone else said, "But—"

Sophie laughed. "To hell with it," she said. "If it's the only way out, I'm going . . . and I don't say I'm going to disappear this instant. I only suggest we go down to the edge."

Sal shrugged, an exaggerated movement of shoulders and arms, and took hold of the handles of Sophie's chair. They set off along the beaten path. At Strand Six more people joined them, and at Strand Two more. Runners went off to spread the word: By the time they reached the river's edge, Strand One was already waiting for them. As they followed the river, a glimmer of light began to show.

"Let's stop here," J2 said. "Please, Sophie."

"So near and yet so far?" Sophie said, but before J2 could answer, Mike said, "Ssh! Listen."

They listened. Gem could hear the blood pulsing in her ears. It grew louder. Someone was wading upstream from the arch where the river came out.

They waited. Nearer, nearer.

"What do you want?" Sophie called.

"I'm looking for a little boy," a woman said. "His name is Joe. He'd be about five or six."

"Joe Marten?" Sophie asked. "Joe Kestler?"

"Kestler," the woman said eagerly. "Joe Kestler, he's my son, I have his name here, it came out of the river. Please, tell me where he is!"

Sophie's voice shook as she said, "Go on upstream. Ask for Strand Three." Before she finished speaking, the woman splashed past them, almost running.

"I can hear someone else," J2 said.

"More than one," said Robin. Behind them the Water-bound were pushing forward, one crowd meeting another.

"The buzzer will be going off in Admin," Gem said, as someone shouted, "Nick? Nick Huang?"

"What can they do?" Jay demanded. "It'll be dropping off the wall, but—just listen how many people there are! They can't keep this quiet."

A man's voice. "Is Owen Smith there?"

Gem dodged back out of sight.

"Owen Smith here. Who is it?"

"Morgan. Your brother."

"From *Admin*?" Jay said, incredulously.

"Never mind," Gem said hastily, and indeed there was

no time to talk about it, what with the noise and the press of people.

"Back off," Sophie said. "I don't want to be trampled in the rush." Away from the sandy margin of the river there was a sloping ledge of rock. They went around and up onto it and looked down. The light of day was bright through the arch: In it people were moving, dark shapes, calling each other's names.

"I never dreamed of this," Sophie said.

"The brilliant Sophie admits her limitations!" Jay said, almost laughing for the first time since he had come back.

"It was Sal's idea," Rob said.

"And Mel's flowers," Gem added. "We should thank Mel."

As if she had called it up, Mel's name rose from the crowd below them. "Melanie! Melanie Talmann!" A pause. "Can't *anybody* tell me where Melanie is?"

They glanced at each other. Sophie cleared her throat. "We don't know where she is!"

Among the dark shapes at the waterside one turned toward them. "Why not? I know she was here."

Sophie looked at Gem. "You tell her," she said in a choked voice.

Gem swallowed. "She went away the day before yesterday. She went Downstream beyond. She disappeared."

"Where can I go? Where can I try to find her? Oh, I wish I'd never— Please, tell me!"

Gem could say nothing. The woman called again. "You do know who I'm talking about? The doctor always said the birthmark would go away, I didn't believe her, I couldn't bear it, I couldn't. Did it go away?"

"Yes!" J2 called out. "She was beautiful!"

There was a pause; then the voice rose in a keening wail that slowly died away toward the sunlight. Gem turned and buried her face in J2's shoulder.

"Has she got any other children?" J2 asked.

"Kate said not." Gem wiped the back of her hand across her nose. "I never even knew she'd had Mel till I came down here."

"Do you think someone will come for—everyone?" Mike asked, and Gem guessed that he had barely avoided saying "for me."

"They ought to come for you, Mike. Kate knows who your folks are," Sophie said.

Theo said, "You go without me, Mike, and I'll—"

"Knock me down, quite by accident. Yes, I know." Mike chuckled. "As if I would. But Sophie—"

"But?"

"Kate doesn't know who your folks are."

"No," Sophie said. "Never mind. And then there are the older ones. Their parents are dead, or gone to City Two, so what for them?"

Someone called from below. "Seven? Anyone here from Strand Seven?"

"Kate," Sophie said. "Up here, Kate!"

Kate Avrassian didn't go the long way around up the easier slope but scrambled straight up, grinning all over her face. "Came to congratulate you," she said. "Looks like you've busted the Ruling wide open."

"For the moment," Sophie said, but smiled.

"I can take two, if there's a place needed."

"Good of you." Sophie put her hand up to Kate's arm. "Kate, do you really think it's that way? The Ruling, gone?"

"Nothing's certain in this world," said Kate, "but I honestly can't see what Admin can do to put the Ruling back now."

Sophie held up one hand, fingers crossed. "Hope," she said, and looked out toward the sunlight. "So much for the old story."

"Which was that?" Kate asked.

"Someone had to climb out the Upstream way before our troubles would be over." Sophie rubbed her eyes like a tired child, and Gem saw that she was crying. "Well, they may not be over yet."

J2 looked at Gem. "I have an idea," he said.

"So do I. Perhaps it's the same one." They drew back from the others and talked in low voices. Slowly, down below, the crowds thinned and the calling of names died away.

"Let's go back," Jay said at last. "Ma and Pa haven't come." He and J2 looked at each other. J2 said, "I suppose I hoped they would," and shrugged.

Mike said, "Theo and I are going out this way." Gem saw that his face was lit from within by some immense happiness. He said, "My sister came to find me. She's waiting for us outside."

"Oh, Mike," Sophie said. "I'm glad." She rubbed her eyes again as Mike and Theo splashed out. When the sound faded, the four of them sat watching the reflected light rippling on the roof of the tunnel. A breeze came in from outside and blew Gem's hair across her face.

"What about you, Sophie?" J2 asked.

Sophie said, "I'm going Downstream beyond."

Only J2 dared break the silence. "I know you can swim, Sophie, but there is the chair."

Sophie chuckled. "There is. I'll ask Rob for some floats."

"Rob's gone," Jay said, watching the water lapping on the sand. "He and Sal went up with Kate."

"I'll tow it," Sophie said. "I'll manage, somehow."

"I do have another idea," said Jay.

"Let's hear it."

"Come back with me. To my house."

Sophie reached out and patted his hand. "Thanks, but no. I go my own way."

"Then," he said, "would you consider taking me with you?"

Sophie looked at him. "Making amends?"

"How can I?" He hesitated. "I didn't mean to come back, even after I was sorry. But I missed you." There was a tiny, repeated splash; Jay throwing pebbles into the river.

"All of us?" Sophie asked.

"Yes," Jay said, "but most of all you."

Sophie drew in a quick, jubilant breath of delight. "Well," she said, "between the two of us we should be able to manage a wheelchair. Yes, come along."

They moved along the ledge of stone; nearer outside, it began to overhang the water.

"Will it be deep enough?" Gem asked.

"There's a deep channel in the river starts here," Jay said. "It goes on for a long way." Sophie swung herself out of the chair and sat down on the edge.

"Going now, Jay?" J2 said.

"I have to," his brother answered. "What'll you do, you and Gem?"

J2 looked sideways at Gem; Gem nodded. He said,

"We're going to climb out the Upstream way."

Jay whistled, but Sophie said, "You'll do it. Good luck." She twisted around, held on with her fingertips, and slipped into the water with hardly a splash.

Gem and J2 did not watch them start downstream; they were already trudging eastward across the gravel.

"Do you think we can do it?" Gem asked.

All they could hear was the crunch of their footsteps, and the water running. Eventually J2 said, "I suppose we must think we can, or we wouldn't still be walking this way."

"We could just go out through a tunnel."

"Chicken," J2 said. He turned aside. "I must get something from Robin's workshop." Gem followed him and went into his cubbyhole. I must take the tray of grass. She wrapped it in the sack and went outside to find J2.

"I suppose we'll come back and tidy everything up one day soon," he said. "It would be a shame to waste the plants."

Gem shivered. "It's so quiet, now."

"Silence at the end of the world," J2 said. They walked back to the waterside, past the jetty, upstream. Gem stopped suddenly. "J2, I forgot the mesh! They'll have put it in by now."

"Some of us think of these things," J2 said. "What I picked up from the workshop was Robin's best pair of cutters and your cord that you climbed down with. Meanwhile, isn't it time you started calling me Jon?"

"Jon," Gem said experimentally.

"That's right." He chuckled. "I love Jay dearly, but I do get tired of being number two. Especially as I'm older than he is."

They looked up at the tumbling water. A window of light flickered above them.

"Here," Jon said, "take the cutters. I won't be able to hold on and use them at the same time." He looked up. "You go first, Gem. And I hope you can tie a knot."

"Let me go all the way to the top," Gem said. "Then I can tie it to the mesh for you to climb." She stuffed the waterproof sack down the front of her jacket. "My shoes are grip-soled. What about yours?"

"Hopeless," Jon said, and kicked them off. Gem tied the cutters to the end of the cord, and then tied the cord around her waist. Jon laid his hand against her face and kissed her. "Well, girl," he said, "let's get climbing."

With a grin—at the water in front of her rather than at him—Gem tested her knots, reached up, and took the first handhold on the rough, wet stones. She kept to one side, where they weren't worn smooth, but still the water blinded and deafened her. She dared not look down. How far had she come?

The lightest pull at her waist. "All right, Gem?"

"Fine," she called over the noise of the water, and took another handhold. It was getting easier. Gem climbed on, stopping sometimes to feel the pull of the cord and the release as Jon cleared it from a jutting stone. Bit by bit, the bright window growing larger above her, dazzling her eyes after the long darkness. Jon waiting below, at the end of the line. Toward the light, the way a flower grows.

Acknowledgments

The publishers would like to thank the following for giving permission to reproduce copyright material in this book from the following titles, listed in the order that they appear in the text:

"There was nothing . . . affliction" from *Strange Conflict* by Dennis Wheatley © Dennis Wheatley Ltd.

"Who did sin . . . his parents" from the Bible, John 9:2–3.

"Society is no . . . wrinkles" from "On Being a Cripple" from *Plaintext* by Nancy Mairs © 1986 The University of Arizona Press.

"Plan to use . . . 'monstrous'" from *Disability Now*, February 1994 issue, © *Disability Now*, a monthly newspaper for people with all kinds of disabilities, published by Scope.

"What matters . . . mind" from the writings of Victor Hugo.

"It's the cant . . . all the world over!" from *Barnaby Rudge* by Charles Dickens.

"And thought . . . I had" from the writings of James Elroy Flecker.

"And in that day . . . darkness" from the Bible, Isaiah 29:8.

"Then he wrote . . . it" from *Last of the Wine* by Mary Renault. Reproduced with permission of Curtis Brown Ltd, London, on behalf of the Estate of Mary Renault © the Estate of Mary Renault.

About the author

Jane Stemp was born in Lewisham,
England, and grew up in Surrey.
She spent much of her childhood and
early teens in the hospital being treated
for cerebral palsy. She was graduated
with a B.A. degree in English from
Somerville College, Oxford, and then
trained as a librarian in Aberystwyth,
Wales.

Ms. Stemp has been involved in
disability rights campaigning, and also
enjoys archaeology, cathedrals, cooking
(and eating) historical recipes, and music.
She lives in Caversfield, England,
with her pet hamster.